Ariel

GRACE TIFFANY

LAURA GERINGER BOOKS

An Imprint of HarperCollins*Publishers*

Ariel
Copyright © 2005 by Grace Tiffany
All rights reserved. No part of this book may be used or reproduced in any manner whatsoever without written permission except in the case of brief quotations embodied in critical articles and reviews. Printed in the United States of America. For information address HarperCollins Children's Books, a division of HarperCollins Publishers, 1350 Avenue of the Americas, New York, NY 10019.
www.harperchildrens.com

Library of Congress Cataloging-in-Publication Data
Tiffany, Grace, date
    Ariel / by Grace Tiffany
        p.   cm. —1st ed.
    Summary: A magical retelling of William Shakespeare's "The Tempest" from the point of view of Ariel, the mischievous air spirit.
    ISBN-10: 0-06-075327-7 — ISBN-10: 0-06-075328-5 (lib. bdg.)
    ISBN-13: 978-0-06-075327-6 — ISBN-13: 978-0-06-075328-3 (lib. bdg.)
    1. Survival after airplane accidents, shipwrecks, etc.—Juvenile fiction.
2. Fathers and daughters—Juvenile fiction. 3. Castaways—Juvenile fiction. 4. Magicians—Juvenile fiction. 5. Islands—Juvenile fiction.
6. Spirits—Juvenile fiction. I. Shakespeare, William, 1564–1616. Tempest.
II. Title.
PR2878.T4 T54 2005   2004027773
[813'.54]—dc22   CIP
                                                                                 AC

Typography by Alicia Mikles
1 2 3 4 5 6 7 8 9 10
❖
First Edition

For Joe

Sing, Ariel, sing
Sweetly, dangerously . . .
Lucidly out
Of the dozing tree,
Entrancing, rebuking
The raging heart
With a smoother song
Than this rough world,
Unfeeling god.
                    —W. H. AUDEN

CONTENTS

Prologue	She Begins	1
Chapter 1	The Barrier	11
Chapter 2	The Woman	18
Chapter 3	The Coming of Caliban	26
Chapter 4	The Curse	36
Chapter 5	The Lie	44
Chapter 6	The Temptation	56
Chapter 7	The Betrayal	65
Chapter 8	From the East	74
Chapter 9	The Breaking of the Curse	93
Chapter 10	Dreams of Empire	106
Chapter 11	The Promise	117
Chapter 12	The Sin	130
Chapter 13	The Tempest	143
Chapter 14	Revenge	162
Chapter 15	Prospero Wakes	184
Chapter 16	The Ruse	195
Chapter 17	The Reunion	206
Chapter 18	Five Farewells	219
Epilogue	He Comes	229

She Begins

The first thing you should know about Ariel is that she's a liar. Dreams lie, and she is both dream and the maker of dreams. Her work is not to tell the truth but to play: to sing, dance, and spin thrilling pictures in the air. She likes bold colors; subtle hues and shades do not interest her. She paints with a broad brush, making those she touches seem what they are not.

Take that as a warning.

Now, let's start at her beginning.

She jumped from the head of a luckless sailor, who was blown across the Atlantic in the fifty-eighth Year of Our Lord, separated from the boat of his master in a storm off the coast of Malta. The winds and the waves had been so high that the master's big ship had groaned and threatened to crack, but the master, a brave and clear-minded man, had lightened the ship by throwing off its cargo of wheat and had promised the sailors that none would be harmed if all prayed. One sailor, whose name was Jasper, doubted the master. He was sure they were headed for the bottom. Amid the flurry of wheat sheaves dropping like snow into the sea, he stole a small boat and lowered himself down the side of the ship. In the little bark, he began to paddle madly away, toward the dimly seen coastline. But the waves came up over his head, and the wind tossed him in the wrong direction. He lost his oars and was swept out to sea, where the current ran him westward, ever westward, through days of rain and cloud and ceaseless blowing. For seven weeks his boat was blown, while he wept and cursed himself for his own bad faith and for the loss of his master, whose name was Paul but whom the sailors called Lion of God.

When it rained, Jasper cupped his hands and drank the fresh water. He cast a ragged net he found on the floor of the boat and ate kelp and seaweed and the very few fish that stuck in its web.

On the fiftieth day, as he lay wet and half dead in

the tossing bark, its rocking motion suddenly lessened. He felt the sun on his skin and saw that yellow orb's brightness through his closed lids. He opened his eyes and looked down at the water and saw that its color had changed from cloudy gray to brilliant blue-green. Tiny fish and golden sea horses winked in its depths, as vivid and clear to the eye as though they swam in air. But when he weakly turned his head to look behind him, he saw that the rain still fell behind the boat. Behind an invisible line he had crossed, the curtain of gray stretched back as far as his eyes could see. He looked ahead again, in the direction in which the boat was slowly drifting as though guided, and it seemed he saw a giant triangular space of sun and clear air in the middle of a sea of storm, a calm that stretched for nearly a hundred leagues, and beyond it more rain.

The very air was oddly changed. He heard music and breathed a sweet perfume. He thought he was dreaming. Perhaps he was. He closed his eyes.

He opened them again days later when he felt the boat's bottom grind on pebbles. By now he'd gone mad. Despite the rain he'd drunk from his cupped hands in the battered bark, he was parched with thirst and too weak even to think to look for a fresh-water spring after waves pushed him onto the white sands of the island. He fell out of the boat, and the tide took it back to the sea.

He lay on the beach as though dead. The heads of the tall palms nodded and whispered above him. Hearing them, he looked up and thought they mocked him with their high, unreachable fruit. Red and cracked as a lobster, he stayed collapsed on the hot stretch of sand, not thinking to crawl into the shade, unable to do more than roll feebly and babble in a whisper. He called for his master, and one moment he asked if he was in Heaven, while the next he wept and said he must be in Hell. Jasper was crazy, brainsick with hunger and lack of water, and had forgotten how to pray.

So in the end he called on his own dreams to save him, and as he tossed, muttering, on the beach, one of them came.

She was beautiful. Transparent, she yet shimmered with all the colors of the rainbow, green and yellow and purple and blue and orange and red. She hovered above him and looked at him with soft violet eyes, and he could not see that she was a dream and had no heart.

"Are *you* the Lion of God?" he croaked. He said the words in Hebrew, the tongue he knew best. *"Ari-el?"* A faint breeze blew the words to her ears. He babbled on. *"Ar-i-EL?* I am in exile, but the Promised Land lies before me. We will possess it, you and I, and none will stand in our way!"

She brushed his mad, haggard face with her radiant wings. He smiled with insane bliss, and died.

He died, but she did not. She flew over the white cove and called it her own. And for centuries it was.

She was never bored.

She loved flying with her colored wings, in the airy form of an angel. She liked to dive into the seafoam. But she loved best to split into pieces, to turn herself into wind and rain and batter the tops of the palm trees until the trees dropped coconuts into the surf. She coasted to the rim of the Triangle and sailed along the invisible edge that held her confined. On the far side of it the waves turned choppy and gray and ugly. She did not want to fly to them. Inside her magic Triangle, she had room enough to fly.

Ariel sailed far north, then south, east, and west, skirting the edges of islands that had no names. More than a thousand years hence they would be christened Bermudas, Cuba, Bahamas. She dove into the sea and cavorted with striped and golden dragon-fish. When it pleased her, she made more fish, flying things of fantastic colors and shapes, some flat and some triangular and some violet finned and, once, a perfect white swimming sphere, with yellow eyes. She dove with tiny, fantastic sea horses that looked like moving plants, that waved green, graceful shoots from their tails and ears. She jumped from sea to air and back again with laughing dolphins, and for the smaller fish invented games, which she played with them. They swam races, which she always won, and for this she was applauded and cheered by the golden and purple and orange fish, who clapped fantastically with their fins and yelled impossibly, with watery voices.

When she tired of playing with the fish, she blinked, and they disappeared.

She named things. Back in those first centuries she could speak only Latin and Hebrew and Greek and some Chaldee, because those were the languages Jasper had known. The earth was *terra*. A fish was *ichthys*. The waving seaweed was *thrix*, and the sun was *helios*. The branch of a tree was *abothah*. She sang these names into the wind and loved their sound, but most of all, she loved to sing her own name, over and over and over. *Ar-i-el. Ar-i-el.*

She was perfectly happy.

Time was nothing to Ariel. One day—five hundred years later? or six?—it came to her that she could make other spirits, just the way she made the fish.

This was as easy for her to do as it was to do anything, which is to say it was no labor at all. She had only to imagine perfect playfellows, ones who would play her games, and only her games, and worship her always, and there they were: three of them, as perfect as herself, lined up on the beach. They gazed up at her adoringly.

And they laughed at all her jests. One was blue with seaweed hair, and she named him Acrazia. Another was stormy-sky red, and that one was Nous. The third she decked out with the thousand colors of the flower-filled rain forest. In him these colors shattered into fragments and then re-formed into new combinations of wild hues, ever changing—green and vermilion and lavender and cerulean and silver.

And this one she named Fantasia.

Ariel and her spirits did not sleep.

At night they sat on the sands or on the branches

of a huge gumbo-limbo tree that divided the beach from the jungle, singing to the sky in four-part harmony. Acrazia's voice was sibilant and watery, and Fantasia's was a deep, vibrant bass. The voice of Nous was a windy whistle, and Ariel's sounded like all three together and something more besides, and so really instead of four spirits singing there seemed to be seven.

What did they sing? Snatches of sailors' ditties and wine bibbing songs and a few reverent Hebrew psalms that spoke of a God Ariel did not understand, much less believe in, but she liked the sound of the Hebrew words and the music. They sang of exile and the Promised Land. They sang anything that Ariel could fetch out of Jasper's remembered dreams, although Jasper himself was by now only bones on the beach. Some of those bones had been deep buried by sand, but some the spirits uncovered and knocked together to help their music. They hollowed out coconuts and pounded them mercilessly with the remains of poor Jasper, yelling, "Tibia, fibia, tibia, fibia," and then they howled at the moon.

When Ariel tired of her spirits' singing, she blinked, and they vanished for a time.

．　　　．　　　．

She and her minions kept to the cove, though there came a day, a seasonless century later, when from far inland, through the thick, tangled mass of jungle trees, past the island's mountains, they heard drums on the wind.

Acrazia and Nous and Fantasia babbled excitedly. "There are others!" Nous squeaked. "We can possess them and play with them!"

Ariel silenced all three with a wink. Then, rising like a pillar of cloud, she spoke a word, and the three of them shrank into one tiny ball, which she threw into the ocean. "Stay there until I get back," she cried to the bobbing, many-colored sphere. Then, by herself, she flew toward the sound of the drums.

CHAPTER 1

The Barrier

Ariel sailed over the shifting top of the green-roofed island, sometimes staring straight into the sun, other times glancing down at the swaying green interlaced fronds of the trees. She ducked into the jungle three times, to dive into the cold pools and to fall liquidly through the waterfalls. Once she burrowed far into the earth and traveled twenty leagues as a worm. The third time, she shot through the moist air of the rain forest as a brightly colored snake. Since slithering was too slow for her, she rolled at high speed, her tail in her mouth. Tiring of this mazy motion, she changed back into a winged thing and climbed from the dense dark womb of the tangled wood into the blue sky again. From there she looked down on the dark green treetops, laughing at chattering brown monkeys and red-winged parrots. She rose above them, higher and higher. She came close to the sun, and her wings did not melt but brightened and blazed. Then she swooped down and sailed farther, farther, farther, until she'd crossed nearly half the green-and-white mass of the water-licked island below.

All the time that she flew, she heard the drums from the west getting steadily louder. When she crawled as a worm through the earth, she felt the soil vibrate with their sound. In the sky the wind brought the rhythmic beats to her, and even in the muffling trees and the cool of the forest ponds, she heard the drums pounding, pounding, pounding. Her brain throbbed with their sound.

At the midpoint of the island she stopped and hovered in midair. Her wings beat like the wings of a dragonfly, and they hummed. She was high above the forest, and ahead she could just see the white hem of the beach that ringed the island, on the far part, where she had never been. She heard the ocean waves and saw them, blue-gray with white fringe, as they crashed on that distant shore.

She frowned. For a moment her wings stopped beating, and she hovered soundlessly.

Those far waves were not tame, or calm, as were

the waves of her cove. They looked like the waves she sometimes saw raging past the eastern rim of the Triangle, jagged and high and irregular and dark.

She shuddered.

Turning her eyes from the wild ocean, she glided leftward and saw smoke rising above the trees near the coast, from several parts of the island's western half. The sound of the drums came from someplace near the middle of the smoke streams. It was a rhythmic sound, and clear.

"I will visit them," she said firmly to herself. She did not know fear, and so she did not understand the wall that rose in her mind as she turned to swoop toward the hidden fires.

She sailed downward and crashed.

She was spinning, spinning, falling into the forest, her wings flailing and flapping until at last they grabbed the air and steadied her. Then, amazed at her near wreck, she rose high again, above the trees, to see what had stopped her.

There was nothing to see, nothing but the same far beach with the gray, crashing waves, the same white ribbon of coast leading up to the trees, the same thin trails of smoke rising up and melting into air. And the drums still sounded. As she flew forward again, more cautiously this time, she felt it once more.

The barrier.

Invisible as air, but there.

"We cannot go there," she said. "We cannot yet possess the whole of the Promised Land."

She was seated with her back to the gumbo-limbo tree at the jungle's edge. Her minions sat below her, openmouthed, greeting her story with just the proper looks of shock and surprise.

"But we can go everywhere!" said Fantasia. His skin shimmered, turned orange and purple and then blue all at once.

"No. We cannot go outside the magic Triangle."

"But this island is—"

"Not inside the Triangle." Ariel folded her wings and dropped to their level. She sat on the sand and waited.

"But it *must* be inside the Triangle," Nous squeaked, "for *we* are here."

"Yes!" Ariel said, her eyes flashing fire. "We are *here* but not *there*." She gestured behind her with one outspread wing. Then she furled the wing and pointed at the sand below her golden-clawed feet. "We are in *this* cove, on *this* beach, by *this* mountain,

on *this* half of the island. But halfway across it . . ."
She gestured behind herself again and put the words
into Acrazia's mouth.

"The Triangle ends?" he gurgled.

"The Triangle ends."

Nous and Fantasia gasped in wonder, and
Acrazia blew a surprised trail of bubbles.

Ariel gave herself fingers and hands and pointed
in two directions, to the left and the right, out at the
sea. "Each of the Triangle's sides is five hundred
leagues from us here, where we sit, near the
Triangle's base. The Triangle is an isosceles."

"It's a who?" asked Nous.

"Idiot! You know nothing unless I explain it to
you."

"That's right," said Nous worshipfully.

"So it's not our island," said Ariel, continuing
the lesson. "At least, half of it's not. Strange that we
did not know this until today. Why did we not?"

Nous, Fantasia, and Acrazia were silent.

"I'll tell you what kept us ignorant, and then you
will know," Ariel said firmly. "Something stopped us
from going there and stopped us even from *thinking* of
going there, and stopped us even from *thinking* about
why we weren't thinking of flying along that line to

see where it led. There was a boundary *here*." She pointed to her head, which became a radiant purple-eyed disk surrounded by floating seaweed. "Here."

"But you went today," said Fantasia questioningly.

"Of late the drums have grown louder. They broke through the boundary in our minds, as though they meant to show us something: to show us there was a boundary out *there* that we could not break through. Not today."

The four sat silently for a minute. Acrazia, Nous, and Fantasia gazed at Ariel attentively, with fit expressions of wonder at her bold journeying and her discovery. Then Ariel prompted Nous to speak, and in his shrill, windy voice he piped, "What about tomorrow?"

Ariel brooded a moment, then said, "We belong to folk of the east. Those folk on the other part of the island have come from the west. They must have, else we would have seen their boats. They may have spirits of their own. Powerful spirits! And those spirits could destroy us."

The three minions sat quiet, changing color, digesting this thought.

"We need men to believe in us, as our father, Jasper, believed." Ariel gestured toward a shinbone

Nous had left propped against a boulder. "Once Jasper landed here, he didn't get far. Only an inch or two up the beach. Someday *we* can go farther than he got. We cannot take the whole island now. Not until a new man arrives from the east. Until then we must stay close to this cove, near where Jasper dreamed us. Dreamed me."

"We are part of you, great Ariel," the three junior spirits chanted adoringly.

Ariel nodded. "And here you may play with me, inside the Triangle. Yet do not despair! Where one man came, others will come. Another will sail from the east one day. Combined with his strength, we will have might. And we will go as far west as he can take us. Only men can break through the Triangle. Our father did. With the next eastern man, we will conquer!"

The three spirits looked awed. "We will conquer," they chanted in unison. Then Acrazia spoke up. "Great Ariel," she burbled, "what is a man?"

CHAPTER 2

The Woman

But when someone finally came from the east, it was a woman, not a man.

Two centuries from the day Ariel found the barrier, as we reckon time (spirits don't reckon time), a sail appeared on the horizon, to the north of the magic island.

Ariel and her sprites had been hanging from the limbs of the sturdy gumbo-limbo tree, which had grown to be thirty feet high, as tall as the graceful palms that ringed the beach.

Of course it was Ariel who noticed the small sail, which seemed at first to be a cloud. But it didn't shift its shape and scud off into the sky as clouds tended to do, but remained itself, a ragged square that grew bigger and bigger as it approached. While the four spirits watched, immobile, hanging upside down from the gumbo-limbo tree, its mast became visible, and below both mast and sail they saw a battered boat. Inside the boat sat a flaxen-haired girl, puffing as she energetically wielded a pair of splintery oars.

Twenty feet from the beach the young woman jumped out of the boat with far more vigor than that displayed by Jasper on his arrival just over eight hundred years before. She took the boat by a rope that was fastened to a ring at its prow and pulled it inland. Then she stood on the beach with her hands on her hips and stared about her.

Had Ariel owned a heart, it would have pounded with excitement at the arrival of this human. This person looked like Jasper, except she was not dying or crazy. Her yellow hair was matted and dirty, and though she had no beard, her face was sun cracked and freckled and not, to Ariel's mind, the slightest bit lovely. Her arms and legs were red and thin, like Jasper's had been, though his belly had been a skinny sack, and hers bulged outward, as though she had gorged herself on fish and kelp.

"Yo-*ho*!" the woman yelled. "Anyone on this island?" She spoke a language that was new to Ariel's ears, and Ariel had to struggle to understand it. It was harsher, more guttural, than Jasper's languages, and the woman's commanding voice was harsh as well. Ariel, who had turned herself into a small purple dragon and begun to waft toward her, suddenly hesitated at the voice's sound and hovered in the air.

When silence greeted the woman, she began to trudge toward the trees. Ariel shrank back into the cover of the forest, with Acrazia, Nous, and Fantasia in tow. The three junior spirits began to babble in excitement, but Ariel had no use for their questions now. So she turned them into gumbo-limbo leaves to hush them.

The woman collapsed with a sigh into the shade of the gumbo-limbo and rubbed her swelling stomach. "Water," she moaned.

Now Ariel looked more closely. Among the images of woman that she knew from Jasper's dreams there was a memory of a pretty young girl whose belly swelled just like this one's did, and who placed her hands upon it in a protective gesture just like this girl was making now. Ariel looked again, amazed, at this squat, grubby figure that sat at the edge of the beach—her beach! A woman? So it seemed. Yet she was *nothing* like the lush, perfumed beauties who had flitted through Jasper's final thoughts or the impossibly lovely violet-eyed goddess whose form Ariel had first taken.

She began to turn from the intruder with disgust, determined to use all her powers to drive her back into her boat and far from the magic island.

Then the girl began to sing.

Her song was not beautiful. She sang something about harvest and rains, and winter (what was winter?), and a hearth fire, and a warm house, and a fiery drink of fermented apple mash. "I wish I had some now!" she said, breaking off with a cackle. She was rough and rude, and her voice was not good.

But Ariel knew that if the woman knew a song, she knew something of fancy, of dream. And this meant Ariel could play with her.

And if she could play with her, then this yellow-haired girl might take Ariel and her servant spirits through the barrier, to the part of the island that was now forbidden.

The girl gave a bitter laugh. "No one on this island!" she said.

Ariel sprouted four wings like a dragonfly and descended from the gumbo-limbo tree. Her wings hummed as she stood in the air in front of the astonished girl and looked deep into her hard blue eyes.

"*I* am here," Ariel said.

Jasper had been smitten with Ariel on her first appearance. He had discarded his body in bliss at the sight of her and left his bones to molder into something rich and strange (so Ariel thought, though the truth of it was he had died of hunger and sunstroke and thirst and had had no thought for the future of his bones). So she was disappointed that the girl did not greet her with reverence but only jumped to her feet with a look of surprise and said, "What odd creatures are here! Help me quick, for you see I am pregnant and need water."

Flying ahead, Ariel led her to the nearest freshwater spring, where the woman, whose name was Sycorax, drank deeply and then told Ariel her story. She was a girl from a far country, a place many hundreds of leagues across the sea to the east and the north, where it was cold half the year and snow blew and ice covered the inland lakes. As she described her land in her plain-spoken way, Ariel saw it and divided herself into a million blowing flakes like a rolling blizzard. Sycorax laughed and clapped her hands to see her.

"That is it!" she said. "You are a good storm. But I don't miss storms. It's nice and warm here."

Ariel shrank back into her dragonfly shape and beat her wings furiously, a little miffed. She led Sycorax back to the beach, while the girl went on to tell her how she had come to be in the battered boat that now sat tied to a rock on the sand. Her family had been farmers in her cold country, poor but happy enough, until one day their village, near the coast, had been attacked and burned by cruel men from a land even farther north than her own. "Vikings!" she said, and spat. The leader had captured her and carried her away on a big wooden ship with fifty oars and two square sails and a prow shaped like a dragon's head.

Ariel put into the air a scent of lovely perfume and a vision of a handsome king caressing Sycorax, whom he called his rose of Sharon. The vision shimmered in front of the girl, who laughed loudly. "Where do you get these pictures?" she said. "No, it was nothing like that. Vikings don't smell so good as your pretty man there, and they weren't so nice. But they kept me alive, jailed on their ship as they went raiding far up and down the coast. Some other girls weren't so lucky as me." She shuddered. "The Vikings were big and pale and their hair was as yellow as mine, which makes me think the villagers were right about what my father was. I never did know or see him."

"That's *my* father," Ariel said, pointing to a bleached arm bone half buried in the sand.

"Oh," said Sycorax with interest, and went to examine it. "Not much good to us now, is he?" She sat on the sand and continued her story.

"One day the Vikings tired of burning villages in my country and the lands south of it, and got it in their minds to sail west. More coasts to plunder there, they thought. So off we went. But west was farther than they'd thought. We sailed for days and days and still saw nothing. Then a storm blew up, a bad one. One mast was split by lightning, and the winds blew so hard that the ship spun around like a top. And who did those sailors blame?" She laughed, a harsh and bitter sound. "They blamed the only woman on board—me! The men decided I was bringing them bad luck. 'Away with the Saxon!' they said. They put me in a boat with some fruit and dried mutton and cast me adrift. They wouldn't kill a woman with child, but still, they hoped I would die." She laughed again. "So much for them. I didn't! I had a bowl with me to catch rainwater and a blanket to protect me from the sun. And I know how to fish. For weeks I had listened to their captain muttering about winds and tides, so I knew a little about how to sail, too, even with such a ragged little sheet as they attached to that bark." She gestured toward the torn sail looped around the boat's small mast. "And what is more, the little one gave me strength." She patted her stomach fiercely. "I could feel him kick. They worshiped a big angry god with a hammer, and they said I was a Saxon slut and their god hated me. But my people have gods too. One is a woman, and her name is Setebos."

Into Ariel's mind came the dim, hazy vision of a woman who looked, strangely, a bit like the pregnant girl of Jasper's dream.

"Setebos helps women who are carrying children," Sycorax said reverently. "I prayed to her, and she showed me the way. I'd not been out a week before I saw land, and here I am."

"And the Vikings?" Ariel asked in wonder. She peered into a dark, hurt part of Sycorax's mind. Inspired by what she saw, she took the form of a big blond warrior, ten feet tall, with a battle-ax and a horned helmet. The image hovered in the air before Sycorax and made a fierce face.

Sycorax's blue eyes widened in horror for a moment. Then she laughed and threw sand at the vision, and it vanished.

"I hope they sank," she said.

CHAPTER 3

The Coming of Caliban

Sycorax set up a camp in a jungle clearing, fifty paces from the beach's edge. Ariel told her there were others of her kind on the far side of the island, but to Ariel's disappointment, the woman refused to travel there. "You can fly," she said. "I can't. I'm nearly eight months with child. And you say they are of my kind, but I am sure they are not. They might kill me or torture me. I will stay here and have my child. And you will help me."

Her stubbornness vexed Ariel, as did her lack of interest in Ariel's magic shows. When Ariel turned herself into a shimmering, silvery purple rain, Sycorax looked unimpressed. "I need some *real* rain," she said as she raked weeds from the garden patch she was planting. "I'm going to grow tubers here. The wild ones taste bad, but they give me strength." When Ariel, dancing goldenly before her, sang her wild tales of three-headed demons and monsters of the deep, Sycorax only shook her head and asked Ariel to fetch her some logs for the fire.

None of the poetry and stories and songs that Ariel spun held Sycorax's interest for long, except for the one that went like this: "Any day now, Lady Sycorax, a boat will come from the east. I see it sailing by, you know. Its rigging is oh! so beautiful—sails made of purple silk, with golden thread—and the folk on the decks are fat and happy and playing musical instruments, and they look very kind and clean. No Vikings at all!"

Ariel had not seen a single boat sail past the island since Jasper's landing eight centuries before. Sycorax's battered raft had been the first. But when Ariel told the tale of the purple sails, any version of it, Sycorax would rush to the beach and stoke the fire she kept lit there with renewed energy and hope. When a week had gone by and no sail had appeared, she would droop and seem less spirited than before and lie on the straw pallet she had made for herself in the forest clearing near the beach and cry.

Another story that held Sycorax's attention was one Ariel had heard among old Jasper's final mumblings.

It was one she herself found dull, but it had seemed to matter to him. It told of a man who had gone to sleep while hanging on some sort of tree and woken up three days later. Sycorax found the tale interesting. She said she had heard something like it once, from a traveler who'd passed through her village. She wished to hear more.

Ariel knew no more of it, but that did not matter to one so inventive as she. "And then the man turned into a three-headed dragon and danced a hornpipe," she said in her musical voice. "He breathed out flames and set fire to the moon! And then a troll zipped by on a flying horse—"

"He did not," scoffed Sycorax. "You're lying now."

Then Ariel sang a new song, of some blue-eyed gods who split the mountains with lightning and fought in the air. Sycorax groaned and said she sounded like the Vikings, and would she please leave her in peace?

Ariel brought Acrazia and Nous and Fantasia out chattering from the leaves of the gumbo-limbo tree and set them to dance and spin before Sycorax. The girl laughed at them and said they needed more sensible names.

. . .

In the beginning Sycorax enjoyed the spirits' company, but in time she grew angry at the four of them. As her stomach grew huge, it became harder and harder for her to walk to get water in the baskets she had woven, or gather wood for fire or berries and fruit from the bushes and trees. And when she realized that the spirits would not work for her, that they did nothing but sing and dance and tell tales, she told them they were worthless.

Worthless! thought Ariel in surprise. As though beauty were worthless!

Yes, Ariel was disappointed in Sycorax. The sailor, Jasper, had lived for mere seconds after she had sprung, a gorgeous goddess, from his mind, but in those seconds his fancy had given her great power. She remembered how large she had grown, how powerful had been the beating of her wings as she'd looked into his eyes in the last instants before those eyes had closed forever. His awe had fed her for centuries, had given her the strength to fly leagues through the air, to dive fathoms into the sea, to burst into explosions of color, to create the new spirits that now were her minions.

But in Sycorax's presence she seemed to shrink. She had thought that a new human on the island would feed her beauty and skill, but Sycorax reduced her. She showed less and less interest in Ariel as the days wore on, and she spoke less to the spirits and more and more to the child who grew inside her.

"I have real things to think about," she told Ariel, who sat sulking. "I don't care about your sea monsters and singing fish. This baby is coming."

At night, when Sycorax lay uncomfortably on a reed mattress, shifting position the better to breathe, Ariel tried to impress her with fancies she thought might be to her liking. She spoke again of golden sails approaching on the horizon, and of a newborn boy—hers!—who would grow to be a lord or a king or an emperor. Sycorax only smiled wearily, closed her eyes, and tried to sleep.

In the mornings she carried close-woven baskets of water to her hut, and each day she walked more slowly.

One day Sycorax said she was hungry, terribly hungry. Ariel hung a feast in the air before her, made with the fancies of food she saw floating in Sycorax's mind: half a roasted ox, sweetmeats and pies, succulent grapes, and flagons of honeyed apple wine. Sycorax reached for a piece of meat, but her hand touched only air, and she swore wildly and hurled herself at Ariel. Her hands went through the spirit, and she fell on her belly on the ground and lay still for a long time.

Ariel flew close and listened. Sycorax lay motionless, groaning softly. Was she playing? Ariel flew to the edge of the clearing where Sycorax had made her camp, near the girl's small hut, and waited.

After a while Sycorax sat up, an expression of pain on her face. She said nothing to Ariel, only limped into the hut, holding her back and her stomach. "It may be now," Ariel heard her whisper. "It may be now."

Weeks before, Sycorax had warned Ariel that the day would soon come when she would truly need her to work—not to sing, nor dance, nor tell a tale, but to work. "Your fireworks won't help me birth this child. For that I need helping hands."

Acrazia, Nous, and Fantasia appeared behind Ariel, and the four of them shook eight shimmering wings.

"Hands, not wings!" cried Sycorax. "Someone to help bring the child into the world. I push and you pull. Gently."

Ariel shuddered. "I cannot do that!" she said. She searched Sycorax's mind and put into the air a picture of a solemn baby with a gold ring circling his head, perched on the lap of a sedate, glowing woman. The woman's face was perfect, and radiant.

She wore a blue mantle, and her head, like the baby's, was circled with gold. Behind the pair stood a saintly-looking donkey.

Ariel struck up the music of the harp as she presented the image to Sycorax. "Can it be like this?" she asked. "The birth of your baby?"

Sycorax looked at the image and laughed. "That? I saw that in a thing called a book, which the Vikings took from a stone building they sacked, near the coast of a country south of my own. A man in a long brown robe was struck down with an ax trying to save it. What a fool! The Vikings used it for fire fuel, and good that they did."

"Why?" asked Ariel.

"It was a foolish thing, with a picture like that on its front. No baby ever looked so, nor any woman." She pointed. "Look. He is like a grown man shrunk, and he's floating a foot off her lap. Why is there light around his head? And the donkey! Why should a child be born in a barn? Even my folk were not such friends of animals, though we did own a sheep. Some have odd customs." Sycorax looked about her at the rough clearing, and sighed. "Though things won't be much finer for me and my baby here." She brightened a little. "At least the weather is warm."

Ariel made the vision of the floating baby vanish and turned to go.

"Wait!" called Sycorax. "Swear you'll help me!"

"I cannot," Ariel sang sweetly. "I prefer the baby in the picture. The one that you plan—"

"I don't *plan* it! It's coming, whether you like it or not!" Sycorax snapped. "And it's not going to be a picture, I can tell you that! It's alive and it's going to howl!"

Ariel perched on a branch and shrank into the size of a parrot. She shuddered. "Well, I see it in your mind, and it's ugly."

"A child isn't ugly! You wipe it clean, and it cries and burbles and learns to smile. If it's a boy, it grows into a man."

A light came into Ariel's purple eyes. "A man? Would he lead us to the other side of the island?"

"He might, in time. But first he has to get born. If I die trying to do it all by myself, the child will die too. I know your little tribe well enough by now to see you'll be useless in caring for a baby. He'll like your silly shows of silver rain and purple dragons, but without water and food he won't live long enough to applaud."

Ariel frowned. This was unfortunate.

"I have helped birth babies in my homeland," Sycorax pleaded. "It isn't hard."

"But . . ." Again Ariel searched Sycorax's mind, and again she recoiled from the clear memories she saw there. "There is pain, and yelling."

Sycorax put her hands on her hips. She'd been splitting wood with a homemade ax all morning, and her face was sweaty and grimy. "I was made to swab decks, by Vikings," she said. "To clean up their filthy messes. That was painful, too. I tended to all of them, both the yellowed-haired ones and the man who was black of skin. The Vikings had rescued that one from shipwreck. Fine-looking man." Her face softened for an instant, then hardened again. "They took what was left of his goods and killed his mates. They were going to kill him, as well, but he impressed them with his seamanship."

"Seamanship? But he wrecked!"

"In a bad storm that can happen to the best of sailors." She wiped her forehead with her arm.

Ariel shrank in size, and pouted. "I won't help."

"You *will* help. Or I'll never take you to the other side of the island. Will you promise?"

"All right, yes, I promise," said Ariel quickly, to end the conversation. Then she turned herself into a dragonfly, whirred her wings, and flew back to the beach and into a hollow of the gumbo-limbo tree, where she brooded.

That had been three weeks before. Now Ariel crouched, invisible, at the door of the hut. Sycorax lay inside on her reed mat, moaning.

"It may be now," Ariel heard her whisper again.

Her whispers and her moans were unlovely, like most of what Sycorax did. Bored, Ariel flew to the beach. There she turned herself into a four-armed, blue-feathered sprite with the head of a cat. She picked up the splintery remains of Jasper's thighbone and summoned Acrazia, Nous, and Fantasia to appear, joined, in the form of a ball. With the bone she knocked them into the water, where they broke apart and splashed with glee.

That night, as the four spirits chanted under the starlight, there came from the forest clearing a chilling yell that silenced them all. It was unmusical and earthy. It was horrible. At the sound of it the three spritely minions flew together into a tight, shivering mass, and Ariel shrank to the size of a human child.

It was Sycorax. "Ariel!" she hollered. "Help me! He comes!"

CHAPTER 4

The Curse

When Sycorax cried out again, Ariel waved her hand, and Acrazia, Nous, and Fantasia vanished into thin air. She had no patience for their chatter now. She listened, fascinated, to the loud yells coming from the hut.

But she did not answer them. Instead she flew up to the top branch of the gumbo-limbo tree and crouched there in the form of a small, winged dragon, only two feet high and waving a vermilion tail.

"Ariel!" The cry was anguished, and after it came another wordless howl. Then: "Your promise!"

Sycorax's voice was closer. Ariel could tell she had risen from her mat and come to the door of the hut.

The moon was full and white, and it lit the fine sands almost as though it were day. Every ridged leaf on the gumbo-limbo tree was clearly visible. Ariel blew on the leaves with fiery breath. They rustled but did not burn.

Limping, Sycorax came slowly forth onto the beach, grabbing the thin trunks of the high palms with one hand as she passed them, to steady herself. With the other hand she held her belly. "Ariel," she sobbed.

Her mind was open to Ariel, but Ariel saw in it things she did not recognize: urgency, and red pain, and through the pain a determined and practical plan to find banana leaves on which to place the coming babe. She felt herself shrink to the size of a cat.

"ARIEL!" screamed Sycorax, and let fly a string of Saxon curses that Ariel thought delightfully colorful. Her wings grew half an inch. *"Your promise!"* Sycorax stopped at the edge of the forest, gripping the trunk of a palm tree so hard that her knuckles grew white.

Ariel flew down to a lower branch of the gumbo-limbo tree. She was still shaped like a dragon, but was now only the size of a kitten. "I am here." She sighed in a silvery whisper. "But I cannot help you."

"Oh . . . *oh* . . . it hurts!" cried Sycorax. "I feel him coming!"

"Don't," said Ariel quickly. "Don't—don't speak

of it. I can do nothing for your pain, and the more you speak of it, the smaller I grow!" She was as little as a lizard now.

"It's not the pain," panted Sycorax. "For that I can bite on a rag, an old shred of sail, if you bring me one. I *know*—uh!—you cannot stop the pain. But the child! You must come here by me. The child needs hands to help it into the world."

"Do not speak of it!" hissed Ariel. "I have no hands; I am too delicate for your task; I can do nothing for you!"

Again Ariel sensed the wall in her own mind, the one that had risen inside her two centuries before, when she'd tried and failed to sail through the barrier that divided the island in two.

What Sycorax did not know was that Ariel could not have helped her bring her son into the world, any more than the simple Saxon girl could have erupted into a shower of golden sparks, or blown harp songs into the air, or blinked twelve flying purple fish into being. Ariel could no more be a midwife to a baby than she could have fetched Sycorax a stick of firewood, or wiped sweat from the girl's brow, or cried.

"I will sing to you," she suggested brightly.

Sycorax staggered toward her with a look of rage. *"SETEBOS!"* she yelled.

A dim murmur of thunder troubled the air.

Ariel shrank to the size of a hermit crab. But she still glowed faintly with the brightness of the dragon whose form she wore.

"SETEBOS!" Sycorax yelled again.

As Ariel looked at the woman's mottled, grubby face, now contorted with rage, she saw in it a great power. It seemed to flow from Sycorax's body, and from the body of the child inside her, which Ariel could not see.

That power smote her, and she shrank to the size of a ladybug. She lifted herself from the branch to flee, but to her horror she felt leaden and fell back, and as she struggled to lift her tiny wings again, the third prayer of Sycorax landed heavy on her back.

"SETEBOS!" Sycorax bellowed. *"Curse this worthless sprite who lies! Give her a body so she knows the feel of it!"*

And Setebos answered.

When the thunderclap split the air, Ariel was blinded. The lightning lit the island like the midday sun, a hundred times brighter than moonlight, and she felt the branch give way beneath her as the gumbo-limbo tree split asunder. She was thrown into the air, but she felt herself falling, felt with agony her new heaviness pushing her down toward earth. She tried to move her wings, but they had vanished. She tried to dissolve into air but felt herself trapped in the body of a bug. She was a wingless thing, an ant with six legs and a heavy head, and she fell on her back onto the split wood of the cloven tree's base.

It hurt—hurt!—and she tried to cry out but could make no words, only an ugly grunt. Even as she tried painfully to right herself, to scurry away with her five legs (one had broken), to crawl like the insect she now was, the wood of the gumbo-limbo tree closed around her and trapped her inside.

She could not move.

To have the body of an ant thrust upon her was agony. To be heavy, embodied, and flightless was torment. But this wooden entrapment was a thousand times more painful. Now the bulk of the tree pushed in on her, squeezed her, so she could not budge at all. She was paralyzed. She tried again to scream, but what emerged from the tree bark was a whisper. In the back of her tiny brain she heard the faint, panicked shrieks of Acrazia, Nous, and Fantasia, and their cries tortured her further. Her minions were trapped as well.

One thing was left to her: she could still see. But what Ariel now saw she regarded with horror.

Right in front of her, Sycorax birthed her child. Crouched at the edge of the forest, with two hands gripping the palm tree, she pushed the boy into the world.

Perhaps she was helped by the Saxon goddess Setebos. Perhaps she did it alone. But the child came, as Sycorax cried with rage and cursed Ariel for her false friendship. Ariel did not recognize her bravery or understand her curses. She was made for beauty and fancy, and she did not know what courage or friendship was. What *she* saw was a mat-haired girl spattered with mud and yelling in agony. Hours later—for now, at last, trapped in her ant's body, she knew minutes and hours—she saw the infant in Sycorax's arms, a thing not haloed like the baby of her vision, but a dark, howling moppet.

He was not a shimmering vision or a spirit. He was a plain human boy, and he was twisted.

Helping hands could have guided his passage from the womb into the world, but his mother had had no helping hands, and so on the way out his leg had caught and now was bent in a way it should not have been. That had made Sycorax's labor prolonged and much more painful, and what it had been like for the boy his mother did not like to wonder. But now he was here, in the fresh air, and the seabirds were calling, and both mother and child had survived.

"You are here, little one." She spoke in tired victory. "Caliban, I call you, after my brother, whom the Vikings slew as he plowed his wheat field. But there are no Vikings here, my brave boy, and all may yet be well with us."

She was exhausted and wanted only to lie on the beach, but she made herself cut his cord with her teeth, and found water to wash him. She wrapped him in the torn shred of sail, and put him to her breast. As she nursed him, the sun came up over the ocean to the east, casting its pink light on the sand, and the mother and little boy slept.

Ariel did not sleep. The sun smote her eyes, and she could not close them or even blink. Trapped in the gumbo-limbo tree, she looked with rage at the smiling Sycorax, who dozed with her back against the broad base of a palm, waking now and then to croon tunelessly over her ugly child. Sycorax, whom she had meant one day to take her across the barrier, so that those humans who dwelled on the other side might see Ariel's glory! Sycorax, who had dashed Ariel's hope to draw from men's minds the strength to birth a hundred new spirits, to grow a thousand-fold in size and spread her wings over all of the island, not to mention the islands beyond! *Sycorax*, who had foiled that grand plan with her garden of tubers and her yowling baby boy, who had cursed Ariel into silence, whose god had thrust her into a tight wooden jail.

Sycorax, who hated her.

CHAPTER 5

The Lie

Pain. Days of pain that stretched into seasonless years.

Her body was fully sealed in wood. The tree held her with a ceaseless pressure, crushing her inward on herself. She ached to move. Bitterly, she remembered flying. But she could not sleep, or dream, or even close her eyes.

She heard the munching sounds of the wood lice that burrowed through the tree and the *thwock* of falling nuts blown against the bark. She vibrated with the wood. She felt the thud of raindrops.

And she watched.

She saw Sycorax and her son sitting on the beach on clear evenings, roasting tubers. Ariel watched as they spread them with honey Caliban had scooped from deserted beehives, gathered at the edge of the wood. He turned the hollow gray hives into balls and kicked them about the beach, limping on his crooked left leg, running awkwardly and laughing.

"Get your arms and legs strong," his mother called. "When you are big enough, we will build a boat and sail away from this cursed island."

At night they left the beach empty. Ariel saw the dim glow from the fire in the clearing, then darkness as the two went to bed.

Minutes. Hours. Weeks. Months. Years. She felt the slow passage of time.

Sycorax ignored her, except to cast an occasional Saxon oath her way when Caliban was off on another part of the island, fishing or grubbing for roots. "A good thing you got stuck in there, however it happened," she would say sullenly, casting her hard blue eyes at the tree. "I won't say your name. Liar. I know you're in there. I can sense it. But I'll have no more of you. Always filling my head with hopes of golden sails and kings and princes coming to my rescue. Did you think those dreams made my life easier? No, of course not. You didn't care! You were in my way, with your fine pictures."

Sycorax warned Caliban away from the gumbo-limbo tree. "Don't touch it," she ordered. "Travel as far as you want on the island. Eat all the nuts and berries of the rain forest, and climb any tree but that one."

"Why, Mama?" Caliban scratched his head quizzically. His dark brown skin contrasted strikingly with his mother's paleness. Her eyes were blue, but his were as black as coals.

"It's a poison tree, that's why," his mother snapped. She had been bending her back to the weeding all day, and was tired and surly. "Just do as I say."

Caliban looked at the tree with new interest.

Ariel stared back at him in mute desperation. But he did not see her.

One night while his mother slept, the child crept out to the beach, sat five feet away from the gumbo-limbo tree, and gazed at it with fearful curiosity. In a minute he rose and limped cautiously toward it, reached out a hand, and tapped its bark. Immediately he jumped back and stared at his hand.

After a moment he smiled slowly. "It's not poison," he whispered. "I could climb it."

But instead of reaching for the tree's lower branches, he crouched again on the sand and frowned at the tree.

There he squatted, the closest he or his mother had been to Ariel since the night the goddess Setebos had entrapped her, seven horrible years before. When the humans ran or walked or sat or played far from her, across the wide blanket of beach, she could do nothing to them. But now the boy crouched not a yard from her. Ariel strained her shrunken powers to the breaking point, striving to look into his mind.

At first she could see nothing. Then, dimly, there came into focus the shadowy shapes of young Caliban's fears. She saw hanging in the air rude images born of the scary stories his mother had told him at bedtime: snarling, flaxen-haired men in horned helmets; grisly sea monsters; gumbo-limbo bark that dripped slow-acting venom. And she saw another image—of Sycorax, angry faced, her hand raised to punish Caliban.

Ariel felt strength stir inside her.

She could feed those fears. She could make them grow.

Especially the last one.

With all the strength she could summon, she whispered to him. *Ca . . . li . . . ban.*

He frowned, on the edge of hearing.

She rested, exhausted, and just as he turned away from the cold of the cove, seeking the warmth of his straw bed and woven-grass coverlet, she tried again. *Ca . . . li . . . BAN.*

The boy turned abruptly and, frozen in shock and fear, stared at the tree.

Then he turned and loped toward the hut.

All the rest of that night Ariel cursed all the curses she had learned from Jasper and, later, from Sycorax, Hebrew and Latin and Greek and Saxon oaths, and a few in Norse that Sycorax had learned on the Viking ship. She thought perhaps she had scared Caliban away forever, more thoroughly than his mother's warning could have done. It would have been better, no doubt, to whisper to him in daylight, under the sun, when the shape of the gumbo-limbo tree was less eerie and troubling. The yellow sun cheered Sycorax, while the silvery moon made her shiver with its pale, thievish fire. Perhaps it was so with all humans, with Caliban as well.

But in the morning he came out to swim like a fish in the sea, tearing off his banana-leaf clout to let it drop on the sand. The sea was the only place where his leg did not trouble him and where he could move with grace. As the little boy dove into the surf, brown, naked, and thin, she saw him glance back furtively at the gumbo-limbo tree, and knew he would come back.

Later that morning, in his earthbound clumsiness, Caliban dropped a pail of tubers in the cookfire, which blackened and ruined them. This took place in the clearing, and Ariel could not see it happen, but she heard the crash, and then the slap of Sycorax's hand on Caliban's skin.

"I am cursed with a stupid boy for my sole companion!" Ariel heard her say, and her son ran from her, crying. He disappeared far into the forest, and when he was gone, Ariel heard his mother begin to weep bitterly as well.

Good, she thought. *Very good.*

Ever since Caliban had caught his first fish, and Sycorax had seen that he was a boy who could mostly fend for himself, it had become her habit to sleep for an hour in the heat of the afternoon. She rested in a hammock she'd woven from a hundred cool, hardy banana leaves and strung between two palms. During that time Caliban usually roved through the forest, emerging with savory things: grubs and worms that, boylike, he ate on purpose to disgust his mother; five-legged freshwater rock scamels caught with strings of tough island grass.

When Sycorax climbed into her hammock that afternoon, Caliban had not yet returned from the forest, where he'd fled after she'd struck him. But within twenty minutes—Ariel counted them, having nothing better to do—he emerged from the fringe of the jungle. He crept to his mother's side and gazed at her intently.

She was snoring. Sycorax's nighttime honks and roars, sounding from the hut in the clearing, were one of the tortures of Ariel's confinement, and even now Ariel could hear her from fifty feet down the beach. The woman was deep in slumber. Satisfied of this, Caliban turned and crept quietly toward the gumbo-limbo tree. Every few paces he stole a furtive glance back at his mother.

He crept not only for the sake of quiet, Ariel saw, but to avoid spilling something he carried in a rude wooden bowl in his hands. When he reached the gumbo-limbo tree, he knelt and placed the bowl at its base.

"Spirit, spirit," he whispered. "I have brought you water with berries in't. Speak to me!"

Ariel could not move her tiny arms and legs at all, much less emerge from the tree to drink the offering. Spirits could not eat or drink, in any case, although perhaps the wood ant she now was could have. But she wouldn't tell Caliban that she was now an ant, or anything else that would lead him to doubt her power. She summoned all her energy. *"Thanks, good Caliban,"* she whispered, and the words floated out on the wind.

His eyes widened. "Spirit!" he said, bending in reverence. "What is your name?"

"Ariel," she whispered softly. She felt a small wave of power course through her from the mere saying of it.

"Ar-i-*el*," he repeated. "Do you love me?"

This was a curious question, but she gave him the answer he wanted. *"I love you,"* she lied in a silken whisper.

He scratched the sand with his toe. "My mother doesn't," he groused.

"*No,*" Ariel lied again. "*She hates you because she's white and you're black.*"

He looked startled, then pained.

"*She was raised as a princess in the east, but she was a changeling. An evil elf baby, put in place of the real one. Her royal parents set her afloat because as she grew, she cast terrible spells on the land. She made crops fail and poisoned wells and spread plagues.*"

Across the beach Sycorax tossed in the hammock. "Caliban?" she murmured.

Furtively, Caliban poured the water and berries on the exposed tree roots before him and moved quickly away from the gumbo-limbo. He glanced back at the tree with dark, troubled eyes.

"*She's a witch,*" Ariel whispered one day.

"That's what I think," Caliban said, sullenly chewing.

A week had passed, and the boy had visited the tree every day while his mother napped, and one moonlit night while she slept in the hut. Today he had brought Ariel a gift of wild filberts, which he was busily swallowing, since Ariel had told him he might honor her by eating his offerings in her presence. It was not true what his mother had told him, that he could safely eat all the fruits and nuts of the forest, he told Ariel. Last summer he had eaten a small piece of filbert that was a little redder than the nuts' usual pinkish hue, and afterward he had vomited for a whole afternoon. So some of the island's nuts were poison. Likely some of the island's berries were, too. Since the day he got sick, he'd been more cautious. Especially, he had learned to notice the subtle difference in shade between good and poison filberts, since those nuts tasted too good to avoid entirely. His mother loved them as well and sent him nutting each week, because he had grown so skilled in his careful harvesting. He had learned to take all kinds of care in his forest searches, for he had also found a swamp of quicksand, into which a golden marmoset he'd once chased had fallen and sunk almost instantly. The sand had made a sucking noise, and the surprised marmoset had yelped and then disappeared. "No more of *him*!" Caliban said, and shuddered.

Caliban's words were puzzling to Ariel. Sickness was unknown to her, and that the marmoset had disappeared into the sand meant, to her, only that it had changed its form and gone somewhere else. What she did understand was that Caliban clearly feared the thing he called poison, and that she could weave his fear and the words he'd just given her into her new and very good story about Sycorax, the witch.

Perhaps Sycorax could be made to go somewhere else, like the marmoset had.

"So Sycorax tried to hurt you," she crooned.

"Yes." Caliban looked slightly confused. He was inclined today to agree that his mother was a witch on account of her general harshness. But he was unsure what specific charge Ariel was making against her.

"She did not warn you there could be quicksand in the jungle. And she told you to eat whatever you could find, and so you gobbled whatever looked good. Why do you think you sickened?"

"I . . ." Caliban paused, frowning, and Ariel could see the dark fear taking root in his mind. He turned to stare at his mother, who again lay snoring in her banana-leaf bed. Her skin had smoothed in slumber, and she looked as girlish as on the day she'd come to the island, before years of sun burned her face into leather. Ariel's powers had strengthened through her bond with Caliban, and she could once more peer into Sycorax's mind. Now she saw in the sleeping woman a happy dream, a young Sycorax, laughing with a fair-bearded farmer as they bundled sheaves of golden wheat, in a field that was bordered by trees such as Ariel had never seen on the island. The leaves of those trees were shaped like stars and colored in orange and yellow and red. Like her younger self in the vision, Sycorax smiled in the hammock. A lock of blond hair fell over her face and stirred slightly with her breath. She looked innocent and peaceful.

But as Caliban gazed on her miserably, with his new goddess, Ariel, murmuring at his back, a cloud came into his eyes, and he could not see Sycorax as she was. Instead he saw a thin-lipped crone with mouth twisted into a snarl, and it seemed to him that behind her closed lids her eyes blazed at him with blue hatred.

"Fear her," Ariel breathed behind him, in a tuneful whisper that pierced the trunk of the gumbo-limbo tree. *"Fear her."*

CHAPTER 6

The Temptation

In the weeks that followed, Ariel lived for the moments, which came sometimes daily, sometimes twice or thrice daily, when Caliban would approach her, bow, humbly place before her the wooden bowl filled with berries or roast scamels or pignuts or his beloved pink filberts, and then greedily devour them as he listened to her whispered tales. A whisper was still all the voice she could summon in her trapped and weakened state, but the whisper was musical and pleasing in tone, even when the words she sang cut like a knife into the boy's heart. So he came back again and again. And every day that he believed another of her stories, she grew in power, and felt herself grow.

Some of the things she told him were not wholly

untrue. They were rooted, at least, in real things that had happened. She was a sprite of great power, she told him, but his mother, the witch, had tricked her into entering the tree with a prayer she had made to her terrible god, who had sealed her inside the wood. The great island had been in Ariel's trust, and Sycorax had wanted it for herself.

"Could you not have ruled it together?" Caliban asked, wiping scamel grease from his brown chin.

"She was not willing," Ariel whispered, *"for she hated all that I was."*

She told Caliban that ugly Sycorax could not bear her beautiful music and the perfume she cast on the breeze, and had no eye for the shimmering pictures Ariel had shown her, of armies fighting battles in the air and many-masted ships sailing at sea and fire-spouting dragons at play. *"Would you like to see them?"* she asked Caliban, whose eyes shone in reply.

"If I were free, I would rule the island, even the far part that you have not seen. Have you heard the drums of the people there?"

Caliban looked nervous. "Once, when I traveled for many days hunting marmoset, I heard drums, faint on the wind. My mother said I should not go so far. She said there were people there we did not know; they might be cannibals. They might eat me."

"They are kind. She wants to keep you from them. She would have you always her slave. It was her prayer that sealed me here. I am not human, and her god will not listen to me, but she would listen to you. You can pray to her and free me. Then I will take you to the folk of the far side of the island. They would stroke your hair and feed you sweet filberts, as many as you liked."

Caliban's eyes shone in reply.

One day a bee stung Sycorax as she napped. She awoke with an oath and turned her head to see Caliban conversing with the gumbo-limbo tree. Though Ariel saw her spring to her feet and warned the boy, his filbert sorting delayed him from jumping and running. He had gathered a goodly number that morning in the darker parts of the jungle where they grew, and in the shady woods it was not possible to cull the good pink ones from the sickening poisonous reds. So he was doing it there by the tree, on the sunny beach. When he heard his mother's shout and the spirit's whispered warning, he hastily swept them all back from the moss into the bowl and turned to scamper away with it, but it was too late. Sycorax was upon him. Roughly she grabbed the bowl with one hand and him with the other.

Her wrath was terrible. She dragged Caliban to the clearing, and from thence Ariel could hear his howls and the fearsome whistle of the branch with which Sycorax whipped the boy. These things she had heard before, because Caliban could be naughty, and Sycorax was frequently tired and often not in the best of moods, since her heart was waning from loneliness. But none of his past beatings matched the one she gave him today. The switch sighed and whistled, and Sycorax cursed the boy the whole time that she thrashed him, though it is doubtful he could hear all she said over his own loud screeches.

But Ariel heard. *"Wretch, I SAID the gumbo-limbo was POISON!"* the woman cried. *"WHAT—HAVE—YOU—DONE?* The spirit inside it *lies,* she *lies,* she *lies;* she will break your heart! Purple SAILS!"* The switch whistled louder at this last, and Caliban shrieked to the heavens. *"POISON!"* Sycorax yelled. *"She will waste us with foolish hopes, and we shall die!"*

At length the switch fell to earth. Ariel heard the boy sobbing wordlessly and the crunch of bare feet on bracken as Sycorax walked, fuming, to the stream to fetch water.

. . .

That night Sycorax lay awake for many hours. No sounds of talking floated to the waiting Ariel from the hut in the clearing.

At last, in the darkest part of the night, Ariel heard the snores.

Ten minutes after those began, Caliban came to the gumbo-limbo tree. He moved painfully and limped more deeply than before. His eyes were red and his face tearstained, and his back was crisscrossed with stripes of raw pink flesh and scabbing red.

He knelt before the tree and hid his face in his hands.

Ariel waited a moment, and then she spoke to the fear she saw shuddering in his mind. She blew it with her breath until it was as large as the top of the tree, which had regrown its lightning-shattered leaves: *"She is not your real mother."*

Caliban raised his eyes. He was weeping. His face was contorted with pain, and he could not talk.

"You have always known it. For how could she be? She is white. You are black."

Caliban sniffled for a few minutes more. Then he said in a gasping whisper, "Who *is* my . . . mother, great Ariel?"

Her answer was ready. *"Your true mother dwells on the far side of the island, where you were born. She has violet eyes and velvet-black skin that is softer than sea-foam, and once she rocked you in a cradle of cedar and acacia wood, draped with scarlet and fine twined linen. Your cradle was . . ."* Ariel thought for a moment. *"It was five cubits long and three cubits high and studded with bronze and silver stars. Do you not remember?"*

Caliban knitted his brow. After a moment he said he thought he did.

"She would kiss you and hold you tenderly, and she never spoke harshly or beat you. Indeed, she was a queen, and you were a prince, her firstborn son. But one day she lost you, and great was her weeping!"

"How did it happen?" Caliban said, wiping his nose with his hand. His tears were drying, and wonder had entered his eyes.

"In a most tragic way. A great party of your people were hunting snark, a succulent beast which only dwells in the far parts of the island, and during the singing of the ritual Snarklefrug song, you wandered. You were very young, and you got lost in the jungle."

"I think I remember." Caliban spoke in a hushed voice.

"Now they mourn you ceaselessly. You were meant to be king of the island, of both its halves. Now they beat the drums and sing in hopes that you may still be alive and will hear them and return."

"I hear them sometimes in my dreams," Caliban said excitedly. "But Sycorax! How did I come to be with her?"

"You were little, so little, and lost, and your steps brought you eastward. Friendly monkeys carried you and found you water and food. But when they crossed the midpoint of the island, into the Triangle of Sycorax, the air changed, and they grew fearful and ran away, back to the kinder forest of your people. At that same time Sycorax was wandering the eastern forest, searching for nuts and berries for her brew, so as to poison castaway sailors. So she could eat them."

Caliban looked perplexed, and for a moment Ariel thought she had gone too far. The boy had seen his mother gorging happily on pink filberts, but his fancy seemed stretched to the breaking point by the picture of her worrying a sailor's thigh, as blood dripped down her chin. Ariel had a sudden idea and spoke quickly. *"Those bones,"* she said, *"those splintery human bones that lie piled on the beach, near the giant boulder . . . you have seen them?"*

Caliban's look changed from puzzlement to fear. "She tells me not to touch them," he said. "I thought it was from . . . reverence, or some such thing. Whose were they?"

"They belonged to a sailor. He landed here centuries ago, and she poisoned him and then munched on his skinny carcass. After that, word spread through the eastern seas that this island was bewitched, and no new ships entered the cursed Triangle. And she grows bitter, because there are no sails. Oh, she is old, old, old!"

Caliban nodded in dread. He had seen his mother scan the horizon, heard her swear and curse the fact that no one came.

"On the day you were lost in the forest, she was gathering her poisons, and she found you. She took you home and made you her slave. She twisted your leg so that you could not run from her."

"I learned to run anyway." Caliban's eyes gleamed in pride. "After a fashion."

"And she uses you," said Ariel, *"to fetch wood and water and to fish and to gather gulls' eggs from the steep rocks where she cannot climb."*

"It is so." Caliban nodded. "She does."

"But if you anger her too greatly, she will poison you and eat you as she did that poor sailor."

Again Ariel feared she had gone too far. She saw the war in Caliban's brain. In his mind rose commonsense memories of his mother's grimaces and oaths as she struggled along the rocks to place nets for crabs, of her rare smiles and caresses—*too* rare in recent years. Ariel worked with all her might to blur those images, while others she sharpened, made clearer: Sycorax mumbling in a corner to Setebos; Sycorax's face contorted with rage, her hand raised, the leaves of the switch bearing down on Caliban's back. Ariel made the face uglier, angrier, made Sycorax's sun- and salt-cracked hands seem more gnarled than they were, twisted her back until it bent and curved like a hoop. And when Caliban turned his head away from the tree in tears, Ariel summoned all her strength and sent that strength across the beach, where she lit the poor remaining bones of old Jasper with a white glow. They shone eerily, frighteningly white in the moonlight, against the dark black of the boulder.

Caliban shuddered and turned back to her. After a long moment he drew in his breath and asked, "What must I do?"

CHAPTER 7

The Betrayal

"CALIBAN! Oh, my son! My son! Ah, Setebos . . ."

The cries were pure agony, wretched and ugly, and although they inspired no pity in Ariel, they did provoke her horror. Why was it taking Sycorax so long to change her form, to leave her body, to go somewhere else? Why was she yelling like that, so tunelessly? For a slow-moving hour she longed for the howls to end, waiting, waiting. Her ant's body felt intolerably pressed, now not just by the ton of wood that entrapped it but by the repeated shrieks of the dying woman.

"Setebos!" Sycorax cried. *"Ah, Setebos!"*

But Setebos, it seemed, had no power over poison.

Stop yelling, Ariel said soundlessly. *It is ugly. Finish!*

In time the woman's cries and loud retchings

turned to gurgles and soft moans. Finally there came silence.

There had been no answer to Sycorax's pleas for help. For Caliban was deep in the forest, asleep in the cave to which Ariel had sent him.

"The witch is angry," Ariel had told Caliban the night before. *"Her wrath grows in sleep, as she dreams. Fear her."*

Into his mind she had again placed the new picture of a ravenous Sycorax, casting aside the bones of a dead sailor and turning a blue, loveless gaze at him. That picture had grown, and inwardly he'd turned to it and away from a memory that the horrid events of his day had pushed to the side. A memory of a bowl of filberts in which poison reds had been hastily dumped alongside sweet pinks. He had been sorting them by the gumbo-limbo tree and had forgotten. His mother had wrenched the bowl from his hand and set it on a table by the door of the hut.

"You must sleep in the cave of the marmoset, deep in the forest," Ariel had whispered to him from the tree. *"Come back in the morning with a carved stick to protect yourself."*

"But there was something I meant . . ." Caliban

had frowned, hesitating, trying to remember.

Yes, the filberts. Sweet filberts were good for breakfast. His mother knew the difference between reds and pinks. Still, in the darkness of the hut it was hard to be sure of the difference. Yet the hut was *so* dark in the mornings that perhaps she would not see the bowl at all. He would sleep in the cave, and the next day would rise early, on his guard, as the spirit now told him, and see to the filberts.

But perhaps he should first go to the hut. . . .

Looking into his mind, Ariel had blown on his fear of Sycorax and his memory of her wrathful face. She had fanned it like a flame. Decisively he had turned and loped into the forest, forgetting the pain of his back in his fear. Ariel's mind was linked with Caliban's now. In the marmoset cave where he slept, two miles into the jungle, she released him from his nightmares and sent him into a dark, sweet sleep.

He limped into the clearing at midmorning to find the thing Ariel, trapped in the gumbo-limbo tree, could not see. Sycorax lay sprawled in the dust of the earth, her stained face a twisted mask of suffering. She had clawed the earth with her nails, and in the black vomit she had spewed on herself and on the ground, Caliban saw the reds of chewed filberts, mixed in with the pinks.

The sight of the one being who had ever touched him lying lifeless in the dirt first brought shock, then a wave of grief that chased from his mind all the fears and dreams Ariel had labored these weeks to plant. His nightmare of Sycorax killing him, his fancy of a soft-skinned purple-eyed princess mother, fled. He felt only anguish at the loss of the woman who had called him son. He turned her body over and clutched its fouled chest and cried for hours, calling, *"Mother, mother, mother!"* Beside himself, he ran about the clearing and ripped low branches from trees and knocked his head against their trunks till he bled.

Then he crouched in a heap and lay still in the dirt by the door of the hut.

After a time he rose and went inside for water and a rag to clean her.

It took him the rest of that day to dig a grave. Ariel heard the crunch of the crude wooden shovel against the sand and finally the grunts of the boy as he pushed Sycorax into the pit.

She was perplexed. Sycorax had gone somewhere else, but what of it? What was this? Caliban's fears she had sounded, and his desires she knew. But his grief she did not understand. It came from a part of him that was not, like his mind, transparent. He named that mysterious part that night as he sat alone in the hut. "My heart," he wailed. "She broke my heart."

But Ariel could not tell whether he meant her or Sycorax.

Her plan had gone awry.

When Caliban came to the gumbo-limbo tree the next morning, he did not bow in reverence, nor did he bring her a ceremonial dish of delicacies. Instead he stood before her with his fists clenched in anger and hatred.

"She was right about you," he snarled in his piping child's voice. "You are an evil spirit. When I saw her, I knew what you said was trash and folly. Lies! I have no princess mother. She was my mother! *She* was my mother, and you made me kill her!"

Ariel was silent. She understood nothing of what Caliban was feeling. She only knew Sycorax was no longer plaguing her. That was good. But Caliban's taunts were unexpected. Had Sycorax gone into *his* body?

He kicked the tree, then grabbed his foot and

hopped about and howled. "I hate you!" he yelled over his shoulder. "Now I am alone!"

Ariel tried to calm him with a sweet whisper, though she felt her voice's strength ebbing fast. *"You are not alone. Free me and we will travel the whole of the island—"*

Caliban laughed crazily. "Free you? How could I if I wanted to? I don't know what put you in there; how could I get you out?"

"Setebos . . ." Ariel murmured faintly. *"Pray to Setebos. . . . I will make you a king. . . ."*

"Setebos doesn't care about you or me. She helps women and babies. My mother told me about her. My mother . . . my mother!" Caliban began to wail and roll in the sand.

Ariel tried desperately to speak more sweet words, to spin more golden dreams and pour them into his ear, but his mind was closed to her now by a wall of black grief, and her voice grew so faint that even she could no longer hear it.

Caliban suddenly sprang up and ran howling into the surf.

She thought he might drown himself then, but he did not. After a day or so she wished he had. She could do nothing with him now. He hated her, and he made her torment worse than it had been. Sycorax had been content to spit at her from twenty paces down the beach. But Caliban threw rocks at her. He spent hours building piles of the greatest stones he could carry, gathered from the southern part of the cove, where the gulls spattered them with excrement. Then he amused himself hurling them at the gumbo-limbo tree, splintering bark, shaking the trunk. She felt the vibrations in her trapped body, and they hurt. Hurt!

"Foul devil!" he yelled. "Liar! Liar! Liar!"

Sometimes he would make water against the tree, which disgusted her.

He turned animal now, baying at the moonlight that shone on the beach, discarding his banana-leaf clout to run naked and filthy through the forest. The soles of his feet hardened, and his hair grew matted and long. She wished he would travel farther, away from this cove; go elsewhere on the island in his loneliness, follow the drums that came on the wind. She wished he would disappear.

But he didn't, and the torture went on for weeks and months.

This counting of time was the worst torment of all.

Ariel worshiped no one but herself, and so she could not pray. Furthermore, she could not die; she could only press her body against the wood in agony and think her own name. She could not say it now, even in a whisper; her strength was too small for that. So she thought it. *Ariel. Ariel. Ariel.*

She would not yield to despair. She was a spirit and would live forever.

She watched Caliban dance clumsily on the beach, and she remembered the grace with which in years past she had winged over the green roof of the island and dived into the waves, and the memories were a torment to her.

You were not my savior, she thought as she watched the boy's capering form. *Not you or your mother. You were not my champion from the east. But he will come. He will take me to the far side of the island, and I will be as great as I was born to be, and together we will rule.*

Then Caliban disappeared into the forest. Three days passed, and still he did not come out—not to rail at her or to shake her with rocks or to rush at the gumbo-limbo and cut its skin with his stone knife. Again she felt the silence of her world and the endless passage of the hours. That silence was its own sort of torture. She heard other ants, busy ants, crawling through the wood of the tree, and she envied them their liberty. Compared with Ariel, the smallest mortal insect was blessed.

The thought that she, great Ariel, could envy the life of a free wood ant simply because it could crawl was bitter. *Caliban*, she thought angrily. *Return and kick my tree! Even a kick is better than nothing.*

But she could only think the thought, not speak it, and in answer she heard only the munching of the ants and the sighs of the wind in the branches of the gumbo-limbo tree.

On the night of the third day of her solitude, everything changed.

He was still deep in the forest, having disappeared down the one trail that led to the deeper jungle beyond. So she knew the thing that approached was not Caliban, her tormentor, when, through the ground and the roots of the gumbo-limbo, she felt it, a raft or a boat, scraping to a halt and then rocking, silently rocking, on the watery rim of the beach.

CHAPTER 8

From the East

There were two asleep in the boat, and one of their minds was easy to read. It lay plain and innocent and open, and in its shallows Ariel saw dolphins leaping, and the smile of a woman who cooed, with a soft face that got big as she leaned over the edge of a cradle, and also the hunched back of a man who muttered and turned the pages of books. Few words muddied the pictures she saw in this mind, and all that was there was sunny and bright.

But the second mind was dark and labyrinthine, and its thoughts were hard to enter even as they floated loose through his dreams. In this mind shone, as though by candlelight, pages illuminated with drawings of gryphons and dragons, intertwined with letters of great beauty and power, with words of a strange new tongue that had in it pieces of one of the languages of dead old Jasper. The words danced off the colored pages, and Ariel heard them spoken, in tones first of rapture and then of anger, accompanied by music. Beneath all this, below the beautiful surfaces of the words and the music, lay something dark and bitter and human that Ariel could not touch.

She recoiled from it, from the hidden, silent pain in that sleeper's mind, and attended only to the music and the mazes of words and the dazzling images that floated above. He was a man, she could tell, for she knew by now the differences between male and female dreams. Sycorax's dreams had been earth and wood, not stardust and moonshine. The woman's longings all had been based on the practical motive of her and her child's survival, and in the end Ariel had been unable to do much with them. But the dreams of the mind into which she now peered were glittering and fanciful and impractical. She reveled in them, and exulted in this visitor who had come to her island so unexpectedly, perfectly, and wonderfully, to free her from her jail.

It must be he, she murmured to herself, her powers flaring with expectation. *My champion from the east!*

And she waited, tense with hope.

. . .

When the sun broke over the beach, Ariel heard the boat rock once more and a sudden exclamation from the child. "Dada!" There was a splashing sound, as of little fingers dabbling in water. "'Randa drink!"

"*No!*" The man woke instantly. "I have *told* you *not* to—my God. Oh, my God, my God, my God!" His harsh tone changed to one of wonderment. Ariel heard him climb from the boat, stumble, and fall heavily on the sand. As the child sang and laughed, she heard the man sobbing. It was a strange sound.

Trapped in the gumbo-limbo, Ariel could see no more than what was in front of her: a strip of forest to her right, most of the beach to her left, and directly ahead the far curve of the cove's end and the blue sea beyond. It was some minutes before the strange human pair trudged into her view, and before she saw what they actually looked like, her mind had formed colorful pictures. She had concocted an image of a tall, crowned man in a purple robe, bearing a girl child of starlike beauty who was swaddled in cloth of gold.

Like that of every other human she had met, their real appearance was less spectacular than her imaginings. She swallowed disappointment when the sliding footsteps on the sand yielded a plain-faced toddler and a skinny, nearly naked man of middle height and ragged beard. His face was nearly as burned and thin as Jasper's had been.

Yet Jasper's eyes had been mad, and this man's were not. Like those of that shipwrecked sailor, his eyes were lit with the light of strange fancies. But unlike Jasper, he knew where he was.

His frown told Ariel that.

He had dried his tears and finished his prayerful thanking of his god (who seemed to be named simply "God"). "Six weeks we floated, my child!" He had wept and laughed while collapsed by the boat. "God has saved us!" But now, as he hobbled on unsteady legs up the beach and regarded the tangled jungle, she felt his joy ebb. His pace was slowed by the child, who clung to his left leg like a barnacle.

When he came to the edge of the jungle, he stopped in the shade of the palms. Ten feet ahead of him lay the wood, dense and dark. "Is this the Promised Land?" he murmured. "Its image? Or some horror? Was it God indeed, or—what magic has brought us hither? In that darkness, there could be tigers—"

"'Randa thirsty!" said the child on his leg.

"Yes, I too, my dear one." He looked down at her with some pity. "No rain for two days past on that rotten boat. But for Gonzalo's gift of food and our net, Antonio would have had his wish and I'd be dead. Perfidious! Perfidious!" His voice blackened with fury, and his fists clenched. The child started to cry, and he patted her head and lightened his tone. "Cry not, Miranda. Yes, we'll find water! Yes! Yet how . . . *embarrassing*, to be saved from death at sea only to succumb to the jaws of a lion or tiger! Not the right end to our story, not the ending *I* would write." He chuckled weakly.

The child understood nothing of what he said and was still crying. The man picked her up, though he was weak, and nearly toppled from the effort. He drew a shaky breath. "Cry not, I say. We shall—"

At that point he noticed the footpath that led to the clearing. His eyes widened. He seemed even more dismayed by this raw evidence of folk on the island than by the thought of tigers. But the path gave him direction, and he followed it. He disappeared from view, and soon Ariel heard his yelp of delight at what he found: a freshwater stream with buckets beside it, and an empty hut.

She had tried, as he stood before her, to speak to

him, to draw his attention, to make herself known, as she once had to Caliban. But Caliban had already known of her then, had come to her in fear and reverence and awe. As yet this man saw only sand and trees.

She had seen from his dreams that his mind was fine. From the moment she entered it, she had felt a sympathy with him that she had not shared with Sycorax or with Caliban. But she could do nothing with him until she made him know she was there, and she could not make him know that if he could not hear her whisper. As she heard him clatter the buckets in the clearing, she gathered all her strength to blow that whisper forth, and sent him one urgent thought.

Don't eat the filberts.

"Yes, I *know* they're pretty, all red and pinky," the man said firmly. "I nearly ate one myself. But we do not know what they are. Perhaps they need to be washed or sorted. Perhaps they are for . . . some sort of terrible magic spell, you know, and not for eating."

"Wa' *nuts*!" said the child sleepily.

"Yes, I know you do, my sweet. You cannot have them. Eat another root."

The sun was setting over the mountains of the

rain forest. The pair sat by a campfire the man had lit on the beach. He had wrapped the little girl and himself in woven grass blankets he had found in the hut and, with a reed tapestry and some sticks, had erected a crude lean-to. Beneath that he had piled some twelve books that he had lugged up the beach from the boat and covered carefully with banana leaves. Now he sat comfortably, regarding the last rays of sun on the water. "Surely this is the welcoming parlor of Paradise! And yet, and yet . . . there might be dragons. Or snakes."

That morning the two had drunk water from the stream till they both had sickened and then, feeling well again, had drunk some more, and all day they had feasted on roasted tubers that the man had found in the hut, after he had first bitten them to test them for poison.

"On this beach, little Miranda, we are safe from the various animals that might take it into their heads to chase and munch us in the darkness. Loping monsters, and depraved unicorns, and—who knows?—the dread anthropophagi, perhaps, who eat their dead, or the men whose heads grow beneath their shoulders. Let me tell you a story about them! Once I was wandering in the desert lands on the far side of the earth, and there I came across a ridiculous-looking giant who quite unexpectedly bore his head just above his abdominal region. And what do you think was our discourse?"

To the little girl his talk was a music of meaningless sounds. She was for baby songs, simple sentences, nursery tales. Yet her father kept on, as though addressing some learned person. He seemed to have no idea how to talk to a child.

In time, lulled by his polysyllabic babble, the little one fell asleep, with her head resting on his lap. After a while he fell silent and let his own head drop to his chest.

Ariel waited. Night was the time when fancies rode forth from the human mind, to greet the darkness. At night his mind would open widely to her.

The velvet sky deepened, and the moon rose.

She began by saying not his name but her own.

When she had cast her strongest whisper and he still sat with his head bowed, she feared he was praying. Sycorax's mind had been a hard nut to crack at any hour of the day or night, but during the rare occasions when she'd prayed to Setebos, it had sealed itself up like an iron fort, impervious to any of Ariel's attempts to invade it. If this man was praying to the god he called God, it would be hard indeed to work him to her will, perhaps impossible.

But he was not praying, or if he was, it was without much concentration. For in a minute or so, to her relief, her whisper was answered by his thought.

Is it you? he said in his mind. Then his back straightened, and his eyes popped open, in excitement or fear, and he spoke aloud. "Who speaks? *Where are you?*"

"Over here." Her whisper grew stronger at his response. *"In the gumbo-limbo tree."*

By good fortune, the wind blew at just that moment, and the remaining leaves of the big tree rustled, louder than those of the palms.

He jumped up, toppling his baby's head into the sand. The child turned over, sturdy and unperturbed, and said, "Gobble." In her head Ariel saw dancing ducks and a flying sugarsop.

She turned her attention back to the man and again saw, behind his lined forehead, the maze of thoughts, of letters and words and pictures and musical notes, and beneath it all, the darkness.

As his mind turned itself toward her, groping, reaching, she sensed in it a power of fancy greater than any she had ever known. His thoughts met hers, and she felt her own strength stir.

"I am here," she breathed to him. *"Fear not. I am Ariel, and I am here."* Her voice came like the waves that crashed onto the sand.

He let his grass blanket slip to the ground and cocked his head. "The voice!" he murmured. "I am sure I have not heard it before, and yet it is . . . familiar. . . ."

"I am Ariel. Come to me."

Barefoot, and clad only in the ragged remains of his cloth breeches, he walked to the tree.

Ariel expected him to kneel before it, as Caliban had. But he stood erect. If the gumbo-limbo had had eyes—which, in fact, it had, since her own eyes were in it—he would have been facing it eye to eye.

"I am Prospero," he said sternly. "And who or what is the spirit that borrows the tongue of ancient Israel and calls itself the Lion of God?"

The night had entered its darkest phase when Prospero sat back on his heels and said, "So." He rose and went to stoke the fire, then returned with a torch. By its light his face looked shadowed and ghostly. "So," he said again.

She had told him her story, and in his canniness

83

he had made her tell him more of the truth than she'd told young Caliban. He now knew the manner of her birth and of her imprisonment in the tree, if not the exact reasons Sycorax had been angry with her. But she'd said nothing of Caliban yet. Perhaps, after all, there was no need to speak of that vile little boy. He might have met beasts in the forest or, hungry in his wanderings, have gobbled the wrong filbert in the darkness of a culvert and met the fate of his mother.

She hoped so.

Though the man Prospero wondered at her tale, he believed it, too, not only because her voice was clearly there, in the darkness, speaking to him, but because he himself had noted the Triangle that began many leagues out to sea, the shape she said ended trackless leagues into the forest, in the middle of the island.

"So," he said a third time now, as he steadied the base of his torch in the sand. "A Triangle. Yes. There was something . . . a line that, in a moment, changed everything—the sky and the water and the air, out there." He pointed, believing the spirit he still could not see could mark his gesture, as indeed she could. "Behind us it rained, and where we sailed, on the near side of an invisible barrier, all was sunny and blue. Even the baby knew it. She said the air smelled like candy. Yes, there is strange magic in this region."

"I am the magic."

"Hmm. You are *of* the magic, I think. But if you *were* the magic, you could let yourself out of that tree, could you not?"

She was silent. Once more she felt the strange force of his mind, which fused logic with boundless fantasy.

"No-ho-ho," he said. "I believe you are inclined to deceive, my tricksy spirit. I feel I know you. No, you are not all the magic there is in the world. You cannot let yourself out. You'll need me to do it for you."

"Can you do it?" she asked. *"Who are you?"*

"Two questions. I shall answer the last first. I am a, er—"

"Prince?"

"Ah, yes. A prince of some note, in my far country, which is called Milan. A duke, in fact. I was tricked and betrayed by my brother." His voice grew dark, and his fist clenched a handful of sand. He shook the fist and let the grains fall in scatterings back to the earth. "Antonio. He craved my . . ." He paused.

Again Ariel saw the darkness in his thought.

He'd gone suddenly awash in a wordless, bitter confusion. She looked hard into his throbbing memories and saw another man's face, darkly bearded, and a woman's, weeping. She saw a flash of red grief, and then the picture of the dilapidated sailboat that now lay beached on the island shore.

"He craved your throne and your lady," she whispered helpfully. *"He put you into a rotten boat and set you adrift to get rid of you forever."*

His brow furrowed in perplexity. "Did he so?" he said softly. "Yes . . . yes, so it must have been. Yes! We were putting into port, far from home, all of us, at Lisbon, where we had come on a—" He frowned again. "Now, why were we there?'

He was not stark mad, as Jasper had been, but he had spent weeks drifting in a boat, nursing grief, fretting for the child, and fighting despair, and now breathed the dreamy air of the magic island. And when he mentioned his brother, Antonio, his thoughts shifted—Ariel saw them shift—and he began to speak out of the dark thing in his mind. That dark thing seemed to unsettle his wits a little.

Yet his darkness, too, could work to Ariel's purpose. When Caliban had worshiped her, she had grown stronger with every word he had said to her.

Now, restrengthened by Prospero, she used her heightened powers to peer harder into the shadows at the back of his brain. She saw dim shapes. Again, the black-bearded man's face and the woman's, weeping. Now, a third man's face. And the face of a—

Cow?

She had seen cows before, in the memories of Sycorax. A cow would not do. She must alter this cud-chewing beast into something more interesting; put a lovelier or scarier picture in its place. She knew she must paint bold pictures for this man, to enhance whatever angry dream he had harbored for weeks as he had rocked in his desperate little boat. She would do this and put him in a temper to free her so as to augment his own power and improve his castaway status.

For she could do many spectacular things for him. She would show him that, as soon as he gave her liberty.

Though she could not yet see what had really driven him across the seas to her, she did not care about the truth. As always, she cared for a good story, and she knew this much of Prospero already: he liked stories, too.

So she fanned the flames of his fantasy. *"Your brother tricked you when you were on a visit of state. A journey to the court of a monarch."*

"Just so." Prospero nodded. "Yes! And he made a pact with that monarch. It was *then* he sealed his betrayal. The two of them saw to it that I was cast adrift on the seas, and thought dead, that he might take my duchess and my—"

"Throne!"

"Yes. Cast on the seas! Myself and my daughter! A girl of three!" His voice grew hot. "A thing never to be forgiven."

"You have lost everything," sang Ariel soothingly. *"But you live. And you have met me, me, me."*

Once he had freed her, she would tell this man of sorrows the rest of her secret, of the new realm that awaited him if he wanted it. With her at his side, he would conquer and rule the whole island.

But she would not say everything at once. In a well-spun tale, each thing had its place.

"I have met you, yes," Prospero said, "and you may rejoice that you have met *me*. There are men, do you know, who do not believe in tree spirits, or who think that if such things do exist, they are not at all worthwhile."

"Some women think the same," whispered Ariel, recalling Sycorax's blue scowl as she'd spat at the gumbo-limbo tree.

"I believe in spirits, however. I myself am a magician of some skill." Prospero did not explain why his skill had not saved him from his brother's treachery, and Ariel did not care to ask, so eager was she to believe *him*. "I can free you," he went on quickly, "but I will not do it before you tell me the thing you are hiding."

She looked into his mind and saw he was thinking of the empty hut and the bowl of unsorted filberts.

"Who lives by this cove?" he asked, "and what is your traffic with him?"

"A black monster lives here," she answered without hesitation. Into his mind she blew an image of a dark, lurching, apelike thing. He shuddered. *"A monster child!"* she went on. *"Son of the witch, who torments me more than she did. A hellion who poisoned his own mother, out of malice and the desire to rule the island. He is traveling through the forest now, looking for poisons to put in his potions. It was well you did not eat the stuff you found in his hut! Save for the tubers, which he eats to live, those things are the venomous*

fruits he used to make Sycorax leave her body and go away. They would have done the same to you. It was I who warned you. I, Ariel. Ariel. Ariel."

He looked gravely at the tree. "I *did* hear a warning, Ariel. That is why I was not surprised to hear you speak tonight. I knew there was . . . someone here. A kind spirit . . ."

Ariel hummed a snatch of sweet music, and he smiled.

"I was starving when I broke into the hut; I had a nut at my lips when I heard you. I thank you. I must trust you." He leaned closer to the tree, excitement growing in his face. "I think you yourself do not fully understand who you are. You speak of a lost sailor from whose mind you sprang. What you say of him makes me believe he was a follower of a great saint, an apostle of our Lord. Perhaps this Jasper had even seen the Christ when he walked on this earth."

"He spoke that name," breathed Ariel.

"The man whom your Jasper followed was a man we now call Saint Paul. I will tell you of his travels one day. Earthquakes and tempest! They make a good story. His followers called him what you call yourself. *Ar-i-el.* Lion of God. You're a holy namesake, Ariel."

"That is most interesting," Ariel crooned. In fact, she thought it was absurd. *She* was Ariel. No one else. But of course she did not betray these thoughts to Prospero. To flatter him was important.

For he had said he would get her out.

"No. I said I *could* get you out," he corrected her. She was stunned.

It was her province to read thoughts. No human had ever before read hers! And yet her knowledge of humans was not great. Was there more to them than she had seen in Caliban, in Sycorax; in Jasper, whom she'd known for mere minutes before his spirit fled his body? Could humans vie with spirits in understanding? What *was* this man? She had felt the might of his fancy, which much surpassed that of Sycorax. Was he, after all, a fellow spirit? Though how could a spirit look so . . . *unpromising*?

Awash in her wonderings, she forgot that she herself now wore the lowly body of a broken-legged wood ant.

"I am no spirit," he said. "I am merely intuitive, my Ariel. That means—"

"I know what it means," she whispered, showing her irritation before she could stop herself. *"It means you are a good guesser. I know all the words you know.*

I speak Hebrew, Greek, Latin, and Saxon, and I can curse in Norse. And now I know your Milanese and all your other dialects. I know everything you know."

"Oh, do you?" His voice was amused. And again she glimpsed in the recesses of his brain a darkness she could not penetrate.

"I know all things of beauty that you know, great Prospero," she amended, sweetening her whisper.

"Ah," he said, and nodded. "That may be true. Now, as for this monster boy—"

"Free me, and he will be no danger to you!"

"You are quick, my chick. Such was my thought. And free you I will. But it will hurt a little."

Before she could utter another whisper, he plucked his torch from the sand and lit the branches of the gumbo-limbo tree.

CHAPTER 9

The Breaking of the Curse

She felt the heat right away and cried out, though her cry was only a whisper. There was still green wood at the core of the gumbo-limbo, but the branches had started to rot and dry on the night Setebos had struck the tree with lightning, and most of the leaves had browned. Within seconds the spreading top of the tree was a crown of flame, its breath shooting downward, and the dry parts of the trunk caught fire as well.

Her ant's body started to burn.

She felt it, a searing pain through the six legs (one broken) and the tiny ant's trunk and the heavy ant's head, felt ant's blood boiling and skin popping, felt the pain of the mortal thing.

But she was not mortal, as Prospero knew. As the

tree's trunk buckled and blackened, and her body was consumed by ash, Ariel rose up, borrowing tongues of fire to crown her head, which swelled, majestic and huge, with purple eyes and rainbow hair. She cried her triumph in the voice of twenty trumpets.

She was stronger than she had ever been in her life.

"LIBERTAS!" she yelled. "FREEDOM!"

Prospero stood back in awe and nearly fell to his knees, though he steadied himself. Then a gust of hot wind shook him, and he toppled onto his backside in the sand. The orange light of the growing fire lit his face, and as Ariel's breath blew his hair, it formed a stiff halo around his head. He looked like a shaman, a wizard, or a saint.

He pulled himself to his feet and stared, wide-eyed, at the fire. The burning gumbo-limbo stood some yards from the line of palms, but Ariel's rising had brought a wind, and now the fire was growing, spreading to the outer edge of the forest, mingling its roar with the popping of tree trunks.

A new blast of wind shook Prospero, so strong and hot that it threw him again to the sand. Once more he righted himself, never taking his eyes off Ariel and the fire in which she sported. Ariel turned the flames blue and pink and purple and spread her wings until they reached a twenty-foot span. *"I am free!"*

Prospero clapped his hands wildly and jumped up and down like a child. "Oh, marvels! Wonders, wonders!! But ah, God and Mary and all the saints, the island will burn to a wreck!" He looked frantically behind him at his boat, and then, as though struck by a sudden memory, at the baby, who still lay soundly sleeping beneath the lean-to. Then his eyes widened as he looked past her into the lean-to. "My books!" He ran to gather the pile of damp volumes, then, checking himself, raised the child's sleeping form instead. *"Stupid me!"* With his other arm he picked up six books and ran with the burdens to his boat, where he placed them, the child still sleeping, in the prow.

From there, near the shoreline, he turned to Ariel, who was now doing cartwheels in the air above the multicolored flames.

She had known power before she'd been trapped in the tree, but *this!* Prospero's delight in her tricks gave her strength beyond any she herself had dreamed of possessing. Fired by his fancy, she flew higher and higher, her wings broadening until they blocked the moon from Prospero's view. *Rich and strange!* She sent a shower of blue and green sparks down toward his upturned face, then cooled them into sand before they reached him, to keep him from harm. He laughed and raised his fists as though her freedom were his own, forgetting his and his daughter's danger.

She sailed higher still.

The flames grew.

A quarter mile of forest was burning, and the fire now reached fifty feet up into the starry sky.

Miranda turned in her sleep, nudging her father's foot. He looked down in sudden concern, then cupped his hands and yelled, *"I beg you, brave spirit! I have released you! Do not kill us!"*

A giant palm exploded. Miranda awoke, sat up, looked at the towering flames, and laughed and clapped her hands as her father had. "More!" she cried. "More, more!"

His glee fading, Prospero clutched his head with his hands. "I did not plan this well, did not plan this well at all," he moaned. "My child, I fear we must put to sea again; there are other islands hereabouts; perhaps we might reach one; perhaps their natives are friendly—"

"Do you not like it?" cried Ariel, swooping down

and brushing his face with her wings. "I can change the colors, noble duke!" She flew high and pointed her wings, and the flames were suddenly striped with green. She sang a piercing chord, three notes in one, and there in the air, also singing, were Acrazia and Nous and Fantasia, aflame in colors of blue and red and purple, rolling and tumbling and laughing above the palms.

"I *love* it!" Prospero yelled back, mopping his face. He raised his arms and shook them. "'Tis *glorious*! But ah, dear God, it will make a wasteland, and—" He glanced at a leaky bucket in the boat, and bent and picked it up, saying, "Oh, hell . . ."

Ariel clapped her wings together, and a blast of thunder shook the air. Immediately rain began pelting down in fat, fast drops. She shook her head and roared in triumph.

For it was real rain.

Within the space of a minute the flames were doused. Ariel and her three spirits flew above the charred palms and the logwood trees behind them and restored their greenery, as Prospero watched, gaping, the bucket in his hands, and Miranda laughed and clapped louder. As Ariel flew, turning somersaults and cartwheels in the air, the moon above the island brightened and the beach shone white. In a trice the trees were whole again, waving their heads in a calm breeze.

All, that is, save the gumbo-limbo tree, which stood alone, a charred ruin, at the edge of the wood, blackly smoldering, refusing to be enlivened.

Ariel alighted at the water's edge near Prospero, shrank her size to his, folded her wings, and approached him. She grew olive-green arms and orange hands and passed a palm over the head of Miranda, whose giggles had begun to irk her. "Sleep," she said. "Remember nothing." Immediately the child began to snore.

Prospero's brown eyes threatened to jump from his skull. Wonder filled them, yet despite the awe with which they shone, there still lurked in them a canniness. He and Ariel regarded each other in silence for some minutes, as Miranda snored babylike and the waves lapped peacefully on the sand.

"Well," he said at length, "I can see you are a spirit to be reckoned with, Ariel. Yet I must not worship you. That would be idolatry. Instead I must make you my servant, and *do not forget*"—he wagged a forefinger at the spirit, who had drawn herself up in proud anger—"I who released you can shrink you and close you up again, if not in that ruined tree, then in another. I came from the east, like the witch who first confined you. You will find service to me sweeter than a wooden jail."

Ariel said nothing, but her mind raced like lightning. Surely what he said was so. She should heed him.

She could think of this as a game. She liked games and was good at them. She would say she was serving him.

But he had feared she would kill them, and that proved that, for all his mind's power, he was only human. So she knew very well who would serve whom.

Prospero walked toward the smoking gumbo-limbo tree and picked up one of its fallen branches. "This one's uncharred." He brushed soot from the wood. "I shall make it my staff of power. And this tree's black trunk will stand as a reminder to you, Ariel"—he turned—"of what I have freed you from."

"Yes, master," said Ariel. "You are my savior from the east!" She knelt and bowed before him. Acrazia, Nous, and Fantasia appeared before her in the form of three white doves.

"Are these sacrifices you would make to me?" Prospero looked down at the three birds in surprise as he approached her, bearing his new staff.

"They are minion spirits." Ariel told him their names.

"Ah, very fine names!" Prospero knelt. "They have brave meanings. Madness. Mind. Fantasy." He blessed the heads of the doves. The birds chirped, then flew off into the velvet night, singing.

"Yaahaaahahhhhhhh!"

The war cry burst from the forest. Ariel leapt to her feet and turned, and in a moment Caliban, who had raced onto the beach, lay writhing and screaming on the sand. He was naked, and his back was blistered from the sparks of the fire that had burned him as, all unaware of Ariel's release, he had limped homeward from a three-day marmoset hunt. The fire had come upon him, and he had dropped his game and raced through burning brush for the water, nearly slipping into the dreaded quicksand pond in his haste.

Now, as he thrashed about, he cried out, "I must get to the sea! I must go to the water!" In his language this was something like *"Mere straeta! Mundon brugdum!"* but to Prospero it sounded like an animal's grunts and howls.

Prospero approached the writhing boy with horror and pity.

Quickly Ariel darkened Caliban in Prospero's eyes. She cast monstrousness upon the child, who was indeed, despite Prospero's fanciful tales of men who wore their heads in their chests, the oddest creature this Milanese man had ever seen, with his burned and dark-skinned nakedness and his bent leg. She would not, *could* not let Prospero think him anything but a beast.

She made Prospero forget the soundly built hut in the clearing and the stacked buckets he'd found by the freshwater stream.

"This is he!" she warned Prospero, hissing. "This is the island's monster!"

"Mundon brugdum!" Caliban cried, pulling himself toward the water. *"Mundon brugdum!"*

"Why, what interesting gibberish," said Prospero. "It could almost be the language of the northern barbarians, whose tales I have heard from travelers. Though that, of course, would be impossible, since this thing is not human and since those peoples dwell hundreds of leagues from us, and are pale-skinned besides, while this thing is black."

"Mundon brugdum!" Caliban cried desperately.

"Clearly a monster. I can see it needs water." Prospero was loath to touch the boy, but he turned to Ariel. "Can you . . . help him?"

"But this is my enemy!" she cried. "You must destroy him!"

"He is not much. He seems a sort of pet. I think you have overestimated him, Ariel, trapped in your tree. He can do little to you under my guardianship, and me he may help. Come, release him."

Ariel worried not about what Caliban might do to her but about what he might say of her to the master. Yet perhaps she should not fret. Caliban's tongue was mere babble to Prospero. And the newcomer had needed only a little of Ariel's dream casting to be blinded to the fact that Caliban was, like him, not a dog or a beast or a monster, but a person.

She released the boy from his paralysis and he rose from the sand. He stumbled for the water and splashed its coolness on his blistered arms and legs and shoulders.

"The poor monster," Prospero said sympathetically, watching him. "Once he's clean, I'll bind his wounds. Then he'll be grateful and show me the secrets of the island."

Ariel rose three inches from the beach, glowering.

Her form glowed red with her wrath. "*I* can show you better secrets," she hissed.

Prospero turned back to her and laughed. "A man cannot have too many servants."

Caliban splashed and gabbled to their left. "You *bitch!*" he yelled up the beach to Ariel, in his rich Saxon tongue. "So this castaway let you out! You're just as foolish-looking as my mother told me! I'll warn him against you!" To Prospero this sounded like *"Hibble gibble leoma betcha bracka."* But Ariel understood it, of course, and sent a wave of salt water up Caliban's nose. He shrieked in pain and rage.

"Amusing monster!" Prospero placed his gumbo-limbo–wood staff carefully down on the sand and plucked his drowsy girl child from the boat. "What a night! Such marvels! I do not think I'll be able to sleep. And don't you knock me out!" He cast a warning glance at Ariel, whose glow had cooled slightly, from red to pink. "I heard you cast sleep on the lids of my child, and it was, as it happened, a good thing to do. But next time do not touch her without my instructions." He thought for a moment. "In fact, never touch her. Be invisible to her. Leave her entirely to me. And don't make *me* sleep. I need to be awake and think. I would rather talk."

Already the sky was lightening, and a sliver of orange sun peeped above the eastern ocean.

"Talk is good!" Ariel turned from pink to silvery-white. "I have much to say to you, master." She shook her iridescent wings as she jumped on the head of a small palm. The sun shone through her form, which was now transparent. Through her, Prospero could see the dark bulk of the rain forest.

"You were a ruler, you say," Ariel went on. "You may be so again!" She told him of the far part of the island and the drums that sometimes sounded from there, distant, but faintly audible on the breeze.

He looked more concerned than exultant. "So the island is peopled by more than us three." He glanced at Caliban, who had come out of the surf and was shaking himself on the beach, scattering water drops from his thick, matted hair. The naked boy howled at the sky. "Us three and a monster," Prospero amended.

"People dwell there, yes. Once, on a great voyage over the island, I saw the smoke of their fires. But I have never seen them, and I am sure they lack your wisdom. I am sure they have no books."

Prospero glanced fondly at his volumes in the boat.

"They live many, many leagues away, and we can conquer them!" Ariel said excitedly.

"And so we may." He regarded her with amusement. "But first we will set up stakes here. Now. Though sleepless, I find myself refreshed by our encounter, and ready to begin to civilize this place. I will first build a watertight haven for my library. Help me, Ariel, to cut wood."

She looked at him sweetly and shimmered in the air. "Command that of the monster, dear master," she sang. "I am not made for that kind of work."

CHAPTER 10

Dreams of Empire

The girl's sea-green eyes peeped over the edge of the dune. "You ca-an't see me," she said in a singsong voice. Her bare brown shoulders quivered with laughter. "You ca-an't—"

"But I can hear you!" The youth sprang from the scrub behind her, grabbed her waist, and tickled it. The girl jumped, shrieking and struggling, and the two of them rolled in the sand in a giggling, thrashing heap.

Ariel hovered invisibly above them, admiring the contrasted colors of their skin. Caliban was dark brown, Miranda a freckled golden red. Her father repeatedly warned her to cover her shoulders and legs—especially, for some reason, when Caliban was about—but the girl was as wild as the youth, and always her homespun garments fell from her back when she raced and tumbled about the cove with her friend. By now the sun had freckled all of her chest and arms except the part between her shoulders and her skirt of woven grass. At her father's insistence, this part of her was wrapped with a tightly tied fabric of sewn banana leaves.

She was a large, muscular girl, and faster than Caliban, who still limped on his twisted leg. But Caliban was strong and knew all the shortcuts on their part of the island. He caught her more often than not.

Of course, as Ariel could see, she wanted to be caught.

Now as the two young humans sat by the shore, sharing wild strawberries, Ariel's delight at their loveliness grew, and she felt the urge to charm them with a song. She knew she could enchant Miranda in the same way that, eleven years before, she had spellbound her father, casting clouds in his eyes so as to change the look of Caliban. For eleven years the lad had been comically monstrous, bestial and ugly, in Prospero's eyes. But for Miranda, who saw Caliban exactly as he was, she might make his skin glow, straighten the nose he had broken at age thirteen in a fall from a palm, plant a radiant shine in his eyes, and do all things necessary to make her fall at his feet in romantic ardor. What rich soil for fancy was this fourteen-year-old girl's mind! Were she to pine for Caliban, what high drama, what stirring tragedy, might result when her father knew of it! It would be sport for a year, or many years.

And Ariel craved sport. For despite Prospero's early promise on the night he had freed her, he had proved tediously slow to journey with her to conquer the rest of the island.

The night before had been one of his bad ones, when his dreams had eluded Ariel's grasp. In his sleep he had gone to a dark place of memory where she did not wish to follow, and he had twice cried out, "Althea!" a name he never spoke during his waking hours. He'd tossed on his sea-grass pallet until dawn and then had risen looking haggard and older than his fifty-one years. For a while he'd sat motionless, sorrowful and brooding.

Ariel had watched him in silence from the edge of the clearing.

In a moment, she'd thought, she would remind him of the power they shared and of how great they could yet be.

In the presence of Prospero, Ariel could shoot waterspouts two hundred feet into the air. She could fly so fast that the sky boomed with echoes of her speedy transit. She could touch the very edge of the Triangle—more, could bend it outward into the briny deep and into the empty air. With her song alone she could beach whales.

The more wonders she did, the more he delighted in her, and the more he adored her, the more she could do.

I will remind him who his true friend is, she'd decided that morning as she watched him at the clearing's edge. *I. Ariel. I. And I will speak to him of our enemies.*

She flew to his side.

Perched on his shoulder, a sprite the size of a canary, she guided him out of his sad meditations, back to the thoughts she knew. She whispered in his ear reminders of the treachery that had been done him eleven years before, on the other side of the Atlantic. "Your brother, Antonio, plays the duke in Milan," she sang in a minor key. "You should see him in his regal attire! And King Alonso of Naples still laughs at how his servants set you adrift in the sea, just outside the port of Lisbon!

Antonio paid him a fine sum for his help."

Before long Prospero began frowning and growling, "Perfidy! Perfidy!" as he gulped his morning drink of betel juice and wild honey, mixed by Miranda and brought by Caliban. "Yet I'll net them in time, my Ariel, with your help," he said. "And then, yes, as you say, the island!" With one hand he seized a book and with the other clenched a fist.

But then a look of doubt crossed his face, and the sadness returned. "But we are awash in fancy," he said self-mockingly. "Ariel, my chick, your wild dreams do not take into account certain bald facts. Conquer the island! I can barely govern this little cove." He put down the unopened book to examine a grape, growing—just barely—on a shriveled-looking vine he had found in the wild and planted before the lodge six months before. The grape looked like a raisin, and he frowned deeply at it. "This will *never* make a wine," he muttered. "Never, never, never. Why *can* I not make these vines flourish? You should help me, Ariel."

She shook her head vigorously. Her hair was green seaweed today, and it splattered him with reddish drops, which he wiped impatiently from his face. "Do not taunt me, brave spirit. I know that is not real wine, but colored water. Enough of your games! We enjoy them, you and I, but I fear we need fewer pastimes and better plans. Think of the *facts*."

"Dear master," she said contritely, "I speak of the Promised Land. I cannot see why foolish facts should bar you from your rightful empire."

He sighed and lowered himself creakily onto the sand. "Oh, empire!" He wiped his brow with a callused hand, then tugged his long beard. After nearly a dozen years on the island his face was weather-beaten; cracked, yet strangely smooth, like driftwood. He wore only the breeches, many times patched with a bone needle and thread of marmoset gut, in which he had first alighted from his long-rotted boat in Ariel's cove. He was barefoot and as brown as an Egyptian. "Empire, faugh! I would be happy just to reconquer my vineyard—my dukedom, I should say. As for the people of this island, I hear their drums on some nights, yes, and believe that the sounds are real and not your invention." He looked at her shrewdly. "I am convinced of this because I think you would not even *want* to visit the far side of the island unless you knew there were folk there to be played with. Strange creature, you thrive on human imaginings. Yes, there are people besides us on this island, and no doubt they have a city of some sort, or at least a village. To rule them might be . . . pleasant. But it takes more to conquer a people than one aging man, a fourteen-year-old girl, and a scruffy-looking monster."

"And me!" She turned herself into a peacock and drew herself up proudly, spreading her tail.

"And you. You are powerful indeed, my dear one. But I note that you have a tendency to melt into thin air when practical matters, like digging latrines and sawing wood, need to be seen to. I'm not sure what you could do in a battle other than shoot stunning fireworks. Such a display would impress folk indeed, but when the spectacle was over, I believe they would require a little more show of hard muscle, and some administrative skill, before they'd let us govern them. I was an impractical, er, ruler, I fear, but not so impractical as to think I could hold sway over the natives without a few more servants, preferably ones armed with swords and spears."

Ariel raised her shimmering wings, and in the air shone a phalanx of warriors with golden shields. Behind them rumbled a score of chariots.

Prospero squinted and nodded. "Very fine, very

fine, Ariel." He poked at one of the charioteers with his staff, which went right through the fellow's body. "Let's have that one after supper. Another segment of the siege of Troy, perhaps?"

"Yes!"

"You will stage it in the sky, and Miranda will think I painted it in the air myself. Ha-ha!"

Ariel shrank to the earth in the form of a curly-haired child and pouted. "As always." She raised a hand, and the vision of warriors vanished.

"There, there, dear spirit. Would you like me to tell *you* a story?"

"Some of yours are quite boring," Ariel said, still surly. *"Sir."*

"So Miranda says." Prospero sighed.

"Mine are better, master, are they not?"

"Yours! All of yours start from the stories in the human minds you cling to."

Ariel knelt and clapped her hands. "But I make those stories better!"

"By making the risen Christ a three-headed dragon who sets fire to the moon?"

"It was *my* story, and you made it infinitely duller when you corrected it!"

Prospero shot her a warning glance.

113

"Sir. But it *wasn't* as good. Except for the part about the fellow walking on water."

"That is *not* the most important part of the tale, saucy sprite," Prospero said. "Though I myself have always liked it best," he added to himself in an undertone.

He looked at the shriveled grape once more, then cast it from him. In exasperation he rose, tore out the withering vines, and returned to his book. "Again, I must rely on Caliban to find us edible fare."

Ariel made a face at the youth's name, but Prospero either did not see it or pretended he didn't. "Leave me now, my servant," he said kindly. "Find your airy friends. Sport in the sea with the dolphins."

But Ariel had found the sight of Caliban and Miranda more entertaining than Acrazia, Nous, and Fantasia. Now she watched the human pair talk with great animation, their heads bent together, red-gold and black. She moved closer and listened.

"It's a hermit," Caliban was saying as he prodded the claws of a small crab with his fingers.

"It's not a hermit. It crawled out of the rock!"

"It's a *lost* hermit crab. It came up from the beach, looking for a new shell."

"It's big for a hermit. Should we eat it?"

Caliban made a face. "Hermits are tough, 'Randa. And have hardly any meat. We should go back to the bay and look for clams. Remember the bucketfuls we pulled from there last week?" Caliban freed the crab, which scuttled down the rock toward the water. "Your father tried to bring down fire to cook them all in an instant, and scorched half of them to cinders. He ought to let me cook."

Miranda laughed.

Crabs and clams! thought Ariel. Why could they not talk of flaming hearts and the arrows of Cupid, god of love? Cupid, Prospero had taught her, smote humans through their eyes and left them no peace as they froze and burned, pining for each other's embrace. They wrote lovely poetry, did young folk in love. Crabs and clams! There was no poetry in these two, no romance.

She flew above the pair, spiraling skyward, and roared like a lion in frustration. Caliban glanced up and threw a well-aimed pebble in her direction. It passed through Ariel's head harmlessly and fell back to earth.

Caliban knew of her constant presence, though he spoke little of her to Miranda. Ariel knew that he had told her there existed a bitch spirit on the island, who delighted in plaguing him. Ariel usually kept herself invisible to him as well as to Miranda, to escape his taunts, though at times, behind Prospero's back, she sent red gnats to gnaw at him.

Caliban had never forgiven her for the loss of his mother. He had closed his mind to Ariel long ago. And she could do nothing with Miranda.

The master had forbidden it.

CHAPTER 11

The Promise

That night she approached Prospero as he sat squinting at another of his books and muttering in his chair by the fire, under the stars. The air had cooled, and Prospero wore the robe Miranda had stitched for him for his fiftieth birthday. She had made it of animal hides, dyed vermilion and purple and golden with berry and pumpkin juice. On that birthday Miranda had also presented him with a dried starfish and three sand dollars she had reaped from the ocean's floor, after diving from the bird rocks. A delicate piece of pink-and-white coral had been Caliban's gift. As for Ariel, she had sung Prospero to sleep with a ballad about Paradise, so sweet it had wrung tears of longing from his eyes.

Now he sat in front of his dwelling. With Caliban's help—in fact, mostly with Caliban's labor—

he had enlarged the clearing and built a sturdily timbered lodge of three rooms next to the small hut where Caliban still slept. There in that lodge Miranda now snored, while Caliban dozed more quietly on his pallet in the hut. The moving panorama of the Trojan War had been a great success, and the two young ones had tired themselves with applause and cheering, especially at the air images of the magnificent wooden horse and the burning towers and the battle between Hector and Achilles. Prospero had mumbled some words and waved his staff, and invisible Ariel had drawn it all. Now the pictures had entered the dreams of Miranda and Caliban, and they stirred in their sleep, carried off, Ariel noted smugly, by something more interesting than hermit crabs and clams.

Prospero was always awake at this hour, and usually reading, though by now his books' pages were brittle and crumbling as well as water-stained. Until the moon was high, he would turn pages and mutter, sometimes writing on dried banana leaves with a reed pen and some ink he had squeezed from a squid.

A squid caught by Caliban, of course.

"What do you read, master?" sang Ariel.

"A book of saints' lives. Not as gripping as the Greek romances, I fear." He smiled a little sadly.

"But I have read my romances until their ink is faded and their vellum threadbare, and these stories are a bit fresher. Some interesting miracles in these, and lovely illuminations."

Ariel shrank herself to the size of a bird and hovered at his shoulder. "Is that Setebos?" she asked, frowning at an engraved image in Prospero's book. With a silver finger she pointed to a mild-faced blue-clad woman whose belly swelled as had that of pregnant Sycorax, but whose head was surrounded not by matted yellow hair, but by a golden nimbus. Ariel's own spritely stomach clenched at the memory of Sycorax and the burden she had borne in her vile womb. She dismissed Sycorax's face, staring again at the one in the picture, which was much prettier. It was like the flat etching of the mother and child she had once seen in Sycorax's mind.

"Setebos?" Prospero said. "The pagan goddess Caliban babbles of at times? No, Ariel. This is Mary, Christ's mother."

"Oh." Ariel grew bored. "Him again."

"Be respectful, impudent chick," Prospero said hotly. He had always been testy but was increasingly so of late, likely to burst into anger with no warning. She fluttered in the air, blinking like a firefly, and sang to him soothingly, wordlessly, until his face relaxed.

"I fear you are right. These saints' lives *are* dull. Sing me a story," said Prospero, closing the book and rubbing his eyes.

"I will sing you a tale of great happenings." Ariel hummed, and began.

"There were three warriors valiant
Of great and storied fame.
The first was princely, fair, and tall.
Duke Prosper was his name."

Prospero's height was only average. He beamed.

"The second was his daughter dear,
Miranda, maiden child.
Her hair shone fire, her teeth flashed white.
Docile, she was, and mild."

"Ah, my darling baby girl!" Prospero said, smiling fondly. "Sing on, sweet spirit!"

"The third, of name great Ariel,
Was purple-eyed and wild.
Her thoughts were fed with honeydew,
For she was Fancy's child.

These noble three had minions
That lived to do their will.
The name of one was Madness, and
Dull Reason he would kill."

Two leagues offshore, Acrazia shot from the sea, a green-blue waterspout. Prospero clapped his hands. "Marvelous!"

"Another sprite was named for Mind,
Though he had little brain.
This one believed what sounded good
And soon forgot again."

Nous appeared as a shower of red sand and dropped with a hiss into the dying embers of the fire. "Ah, very nice," said Prospero. "Do go on."

"A third fond sprite was Fantasy,
And he made folk insane
With images of lovely things
They could not hope to gain."

Fantasia came cartwheeling past them, a ball of rainbow-colored flame in the air. Prospero laughed.

"The final slave was Caliban,
A monstrous, blackened thing,
Whose yells were like the sound of wolves
All howling in a ring."

Caliban sighed in his hut and shifted in his sleep, dreaming of his lost mother's face.

"Together did this doughty crew
March bravely through the trees.
They crossed the island barrier,
And folk fell on their knees
To see the eastern warrior,
The duke of far Milan.
In awe they knelt to worship him
They—"

"Stop," said Prospero. He had been leaning back in his rough-hewn chair of logwood, smiling with closed eyes, but now he straightened abruptly and opened them with some effort. "No more of that, Ariel," he said sternly. "No more of that! I tire of your dreams of island conquest."

She rose in the air and took the form of a harpy, wearing an eagle's head and terrible black wings. "You promised!" she shrieked. "Have you forgotten?"

"Get down!" Prospero barked. He raised his staff and pointed it toward the gumbo-limbo tree, which still stood, black and twisted, at the edge of the jungle. "Have *you* forgotten?"

In Ariel's mind burned the painful memory of her years of entrapment in the tree: the pressing of the wood on her tiny ant's body, the agony of the passing hours and days and months and years. She covered her head with her wings.

"I will shrink you to the size of a jellyfish and bury you in the sand!" Prospero spat.

"No, master," she whispered. She turned herself into a dove and came to roost on the back of his chair. "I have not forgotten your powers," she sang softly. "I have not, I have not, I have not. Spare me!"

He dropped his staff. He was calm again, like a clear sky after a storm. "I have no desire to punish you, Ariel," he said quietly, "but you must do as I bid you." He stroked her dove's head as he brooded. Then he said, "Caliban says no good of you."

"He is a lying monster," she chirped.

He frowned.

She could see he was thinking of Caliban's good humor, his hard labor, his friendship. Now it was

123

she who frowned. Quickly she altered the picture of Caliban that Prospero bore in his mind. As she had done at many such moments before, she made the youth's face look mocking and misshapen. She twisted his form and lowered his stature and turned his smile into a leer.

Prospero shook his head, looking confused. "No," he murmured.

Reaching into Prospero's mind, Ariel turned Caliban's pictured leer into a frightening snarl. "Not human," she whispered, almost below the level of Prospero's hearing. "Island animal."

"My head hurts." Prospero passed a hand over his brow. "It hurts so often these days. . . ."

"I will soothe you, master," Ariel sang sweetly. She passed a golden, perfumed hand over his forehead, and his brow cleared.

"Ah, that's better," he said. "Now—"

"We were speaking of Caliban's lies." Her voice was melodious.

He nodded slowly. "Yee-e-es. You are beautiful. He is not. I have always been disinclined to believe his tales. No one so . . ." He frowned again, and she renewed the image of Caliban's leer in his mind. "No one so ugly and beastlike could tell the truth," he concluded. Suddenly he shook his head hard and looked at her sharply. "Although you, Ariel . . . you embellish things a little. I do not think him as bad as you say."

"He is evil," she said. "He is black."

He nodded. "Certainly someone who must be watched. Even, perhaps, a beast. Yet he's been useful to me. A good servant."

"And have I not?" she sang plaintively. "Do I deserve no reward?"

"You have, and you do," he said kindly. "This lost place would have been a hell without your stories and songs and clashing armies in the air. But listen." She hopped onto his finger and regarded him with a beady eye. "I know you wish a greater audience for your charms than us three. I cannot blame you for that. But you may wish to consider a new idea." He drew a great breath. "Ariel, perhaps our help will come from the east."

Ariel grew still.

"Consider it, my bird. The east, from which all of us come! There lies the . . . empire I wish to regain. My lost realm on the far side of the Atlantic, from which the sun rises. Ah, there are fine folk there for you to charm, my chick! A brave new world! Yet before we return there, we'll have this island as well. We'll rule both west *and* east."

Ariel turned her white plumage the colors of the rainbow and burst into song.

"Attend to my plan, Ariel!" he said over her music. She quieted and looked at his thoughts. Again she saw the dark portion of his mind. She had peered deeply into it during his dreams over the years and bit by bit had learned his secrets. His brain was pulsing now, and with an invisible wind she fueled his anger.

"We have spoken before of revenge," he said. "Revenge against Antonio, my brother, my enemy! Yet our plans have been vague, colorful but unfocused. I have a new plan. A real one." He knelt, and from beneath the folds of his many-colored garment he extracted a nautical chart, written in berry ink on stitched banana leaves.

"I know roughly where we are. And I have kept a perfect record of the days that have passed since my crown was stolen and I was so inhumanely put in a rotten boat and set adrift, out of the port of Lisbon. I know the calendar of the east, and I know that on the twenty-fourth day of the coming August, on the Feast of Saint Bartholomew, six months from this night, in the Year of Our Lord eight hundred ninety-two, my brother and the evil king who assisted his treachery will again set sail from northern Italy to Lisbon, which is the westernmost point of the European continent. With them will be sailors, armed men . . . enough to help us win this island, once I have conquered their present masters."

"How do you know this, great master?" chirped Ariel.

"A wedding is to take place, between the daughter of that vile king of Naples who helped Antonio and a Portuguese prince. August the twenty-fourth is a holy day, and the event has been planned for many years. All the dignitaries of Italy will be there, including *my brother*!" He rose to his feet and crumpled the map in his rage. Then he hastily straightened it. "Pardon, dear Ariel. My passions carry me away. To the subject. My revenge! Your powers are great, my chick."

"They are great!" she sang.

"These sinful men will sail to the west. 'Tis a many days' journey. A storm will surely arise on one of them, and when it does, you will cast a tempest outward, outward—far, to the edge of the Triangle. As far as you can!"

"As far as I can," breathed Ariel.

"You will bring them to me."

"I will bring them to you!" Ariel sang, turning herself into a shower of sparks. "And you will smite them, with your mighty sword, as Achilles smote Hector!"

"Yes, I shall! Though first I'll need that mighty sword. Can Caliban make one? I wonder. Then we will set forth and conquer the island, and once that is secure, we will take their boat and together return to Milan, you, me, Miranda, and Caliban—"

"Caliban!" Ariel shrieked, and again took the form of a harpy. She beat her black wings, and with their wind the waning flame of the evening fire rose again.

"Down!" said Prospero, and Ariel became an angry earthbound peacock, fanning her tail. Prospero barked, "Defy me, and I will send blackflies to bite you, then make you a minnow, and finally dispatch a seagull to swallow you whole! How will you like that?"

"Not at all," she sang. "But—"

"I cannot simply *leave* Caliban."

"You *can*," she said. "He wants the island for himself anyway!"

"Hmm," he murmured broodingly. "In his anger he has sometimes said so. Caliban . . . left here as my viceroy, perhaps, when I return to Milan? But

I have grown fond of the monster, and he would be helpful on shipboard. I was little better as a sailor than I was as a—a duke; Providence, or something, brought me here, and I could well use some assistance on our homeward journey. Well, no matter. Plenty of time to settle this later." He put his hand on the peacock's crested head. "Can you do this for me, Ariel? For a crown that stretches from west to east?"

"You mean, *really*?" Ariel squawked.

She was not sure that she could. Her union with Prospero had increased her strength a thousandfold, but even so, she knew her powers still extended only as far as the Triangle did. That shape's eastern rim lay many leagues out on the ocean, but from what she had learned of the world's geography from Prospero and Sycorax before him, Europe lay much, much farther off.

But Prospero was looking at her hopefully. And she had been born to traffic in human hope.

"I *can*, great master," she said. She turned herself into a beautiful woman in a ruby-studded robe, and bowed before him. "I *can*."

CHAPTER 12

The Sin

But that night Ariel sang to herself in the branches of a breadfruit tree, while Prospero slept in his house, and her words and tune were different from those of the song she'd sung to her master. "No room on our boat for Caliban," she sang. "No room for Ca-Ca-Caliban."

He was eighteen now, no longer a boy. Though she cast clouds in Prospero's eyes to make him look bent and bestial, he was tall and lean and dark, and well muscled in all but the calf of his wasted left leg. He wore a clout of rabbit skins and kept his dark hair braided and long. When he hunted in the pale light of morning, he could knock a hare in the head with a stone, and an arrow shot from his bow could hit a running deer through the heart from fifty paces away.

They would have starved without him, not once but a thousand times over.

His religion? While Prospero and Miranda got on their knees and mumbled Latin prayers now and again, Caliban ran on the rocks and swam in the sea and worshiped no one. He spoke at times of Setebos, but he did not know Setebos or think he owed her reverence. The goddess had helped birth him. So Sycorax had said. But she had not saved his mother in her final hour of need, and Caliban was sure that in her pain-wracked last breaths, Sycorax had prayed to her. So what good was she?

Setebos was to be ignored. Not hated, no. Hatred was for the vile, lying spirit who had turned his heart away from the only human he had known before Prospero and Miranda, for the bitch who now tormented him with pinches and, worse yet, with sweet dreams from which he woke crying. In these dreams he ran without pain, both legs straight, and his mother, calm and merry, sat on the sand eating a roasted venison haunch or a marmoset leg and praised her son for his successful day at the hunt.

The dreams were the cruelest torment of them all, and he knew Ariel was their author.

So he hated Ariel with all his heart, and called her a murderer.

Though it was not she alone who had caused the death of Sycorax. Ariel had misled him, had made him think his mother was a witch who despised him. But he himself had disobeyed his wise mother's order, had gone to Ariel in the gumbo-limbo tree, had let himself be misled. He had known the danger that lay in the bowl on the shelf in the hut the evening he had fled to sleep in the marmoset cave, thinking of himself first, of his own safety.

So he was a murderer, too.

He had spoken this deep, dark truth only to Miranda, sobbing in her lap, spitting forth the words of her strange, soft Milanese, a language he now spoke as well as she. He had known her for seven years on the day that he told her how Sycorax had actually died, of the part he had played in her poisoning. She had been ten, and though she was known to drift into sleep during the telling of one of her father's long tales, she'd listened avidly to Caliban's story.

When it was done, she stroked his hair. "You didn't kill her," she said simply. "It was an accident."

He had felt calmed and blessed by her words,

though he had never fully agreed with them. It was enough for him, just then, that this young girl did not think him a monster.

Now, four years later, Ariel spied on Caliban as he laid wild honeysuckle on the stone above where he had buried the body of Sycorax. She shuddered. She did not understand this rite, which he performed often, every month or so, it seemed (though she no longer kept track of time so closely as she had when, caught in the grip of the gumbo-limbo tree, the passing minutes had tormented her). She did not know where Sycorax had gone and hoped it was far. But when he placed flowers on her grave, Caliban gently spoke to her, as though she still lived in that earth.

What if she came back?

Caliban must be dealt with, Ariel thought. With Caliban gone or discredited, Sycorax and the god Setebos would be forgotten forever.

Then nothing would impede Ariel's rule.

But Prospero had grown *fond* of the wretched youth! How, how to disgrace him?

The easiest way was denied her. Caliban's mind was a wall to Ariel; she could not mold it in ways that would lead him to lay hands on Miranda.

And she could not touch Miranda. For reasons still cloudy to her, to traffic with Miranda's fancies and dreams was forbidden absolutely. The painful memory of the gumbo-limbo tree was still too keen to tempt her to betray Prospero. He had freed her. Perhaps he lied when he claimed he had the power to jail her again. But the air was sweet on her wings, and she would never risk its loss. No, best to obey Prospero.

For Prospero required of her the things she did best, the things she had been made to do. Her fireworks delighted him, as did her sweet songs and stories, her airborne shows of legends and wars and heroes' adventures, her earthquakes and waterspouts, and her dances. His mind was so easy to play with, so entranced with the riches she offered it, that her union with him was blissful. Indeed, what she'd vowed to herself on the day he'd freed her had come to pass: he was more her servant than she was his. For she guided his mind, and he asked her to do what she'd wished to do already.

So she would honor the bond with Prospero, while it served her. She would honor his wishes regarding Miranda. She would not give Miranda the dreams that would make her adore Caliban and drive her father into a rage against the youth.

So how, how was she to get at that vile fellow?

In the end she was lucky. Miranda herself led Caliban into Ariel's trap, and Ariel had hardly to lift a silver finger to turn Prospero against him.

Miranda was not pretty but she was solid and strong, healthy and snub-nosed and merry. Apart from her father, Caliban was the only man she had seen since the age of three.

He had been her playmate for more than a decade. For years they had plucked gulls' eggs from the rocks, had swung from the vines of jungle trees, had watched, enthused, the magical shows cast in air by her wizardly father, had crept onto the beach one midnight each year to watch the full moon bring the giant sea turtles to lay their eggs on its shore. Miranda had listened to his sad tales of his lost mother, his jests against the demon spirit who he said haunted the island—a figment of his imagination, Miranda was sure, since she had never heard or seen this sprite.

Caliban's company and conversation had been enough for her at twelve. At thirteen she had found herself viewing with admiration the lean, smooth muscles of his stomach and the breadth of his shoulders. At fourteen she wondered what it would be like to touch those shoulders. And at two weeks shy of fifteen she decided to find out.

It happened so fast that Ariel barely had time to seize her chance. Prospero had sat awake until the gray dawn lightened the sky, reading Homer. Now, at midday, he was snoring under a hammock outside his house. Miranda and Caliban were seated side by side at the edge of the clearing, weaving rope out of hemp, when Ariel saw Miranda's head lean close to Caliban's and her lips whisper a thing in his ear.

What it was Ariel could not hear. But it did not matter, after all, what it *was*. She dealt only in the surfaces of things, and what mattered was what it appeared to be. She woke Prospero with a thought, made him turn his head suddenly and look.

Miranda was laughing up at Caliban, who looked slightly abashed. Suddenly the girl took his chin in her fingers and kissed him. No tomorrows danced in Miranda's eyes. She saw only this minute, wanted only this kiss. He raised his own hands to take her by the elbows, either to steady her or to push her away.

For a moment, uncertainly, he held her.

As he touched her, Ariel cast her spell.

Bestial, she whispered in Prospero's ear. *Twisted, stooped, and dark.*

And suddenly Prospero saw a monstrous, ravening, half-naked beast, seizing his darling fourteen-year-old daughter with the clear intent to ravish her.

With a yell, he rose to his feet and grabbed a burning stick from the fire on which Caliban had cooked their midday meal. He ran toward the pair, who had hastily parted. Miranda unconvincingly fumbled for her rope weaving. Quick Caliban jumped to his feet and did not cower but seized the stick with which Prospero would have burned him and threw it into the sand. He had never forgotten the searing pain of the branches of the burning forest on the night Prospero had freed Ariel. They had blistered his arms, back, and shoulders, and their scars were still there, alongside the scars from that last, terrible beating given him by Sycorax. Now he turned and ran into the forest, the muscles rippling under his crisscrossed back. Prospero cursed him, while he jerked his daughter to her feet.

"Sweet Miranda, what has he done to you?" he cried in rage.

"Not very much," she said regretfully. "Let him be, Papa!"

"Let him *be*?" he asked, in a white fury. "I will let him be our *slave*!"

In fact, Caliban had no need to return to the cove as Prospero's slave. He could have survived quite easily by himself in the woods or on another part of the island. It was Prospero and Miranda who stood to suffer most if their chief wood gatherer, fish catcher, rope weaver, shelter builder, deer hunter, and supper cooker abandoned them completely. He protected them from hunger and cold, and from darker dangers. For Prospero's eyes often grew bleary and clouded with his late-night reading and scribbling, and when he rose from these pleasures, he was wont to fall into accidents. At one such time only Caliban's quick seizing of his arm had kept him from walking straight into the fire. Another time the youth had knocked from his hand a poisonous mushroom only seconds before Prospero would have popped the fungus into his mouth. "See *better*, master!" Caliban had hissed then. "You know these spotted ones are bad and will leave you past cure!" Prospero, shaken by the sudden, too-real picture of himself lying helplessly convulsed and then still on the ground, had not chided Caliban for his abruptness. Instead he had thanked him.

Caliban remembered that thanks now, and Prospero's kind smile as he gave it. He stopped running for a moment, in the darkest part of the forest, and thought. In a moment he set forth again, walking. His face had loosened from anger into sadness.

In the end Caliban did not stay by himself in the woods, because he was lonely.

Far from the clearing the first night of his exile, he heard the faint sound of the drums from the west of the island. He had not heard them in more than a year, and now he wondered briefly, in his despair, whether he should follow their beating. He might travel westward, after all, and see what was what on the other side of his island world. But the length and the dangers of such a journey would be great, and besides, he knew nothing of the people who lived there. They might indeed be cannibals. The thought of them frightened him.

The Milanese duke and his daughter frightened him too, of course. Miranda confused his body, and Prospero confused his mind. The anger and disgust on that man's face that very day, as he'd run toward Caliban with the burning branch, had been like nothing the youth had ever seen outside his most chilling nightmares. What could he have done that was so evil?

He could find no answer to this question as he roved the forest, hunting with a skill that was second nature to him by now. He did not know what lay in those people's hearts. But one fact he did know, and from it he could not escape: Miranda and Prospero were his family, the only one he now had.

He returned to the clearing humbly three days after he'd fled from it, dangling from a bamboo pole on his back a brace of rabbits, which Prospero took haughtily, without speaking to him. Miranda sat by the house stringing shells on a vine. She looked quickly at Caliban, then down at her task again. In his embarrassment, Caliban looked up at the trees, down at the earth, and everywhere but at her.

Prospero placed the rabbits on a rock. Ariel hummed, invisible, in the air behind him.

"Go into the lodge, Miranda," the exiled duke said.

Miranda's green eyes flashed. She stood and said quietly, "No."

Prospero turned to his daughter with a look of rage.

Ariel flew closer to Prospero. She could not touch Miranda's mind, with its kindness toward Caliban. But as she regarded the girl, standing white-faced but defiant, her hands balled into fists at her sides, she saw again that she did not have to.

She could change Prospero's kindness toward Miranda.

So it must be. For she now understood that Caliban was not her sole enemy. Yes, Prospero must continue to fear the vile youth. But that youth had a defender, and Prospero must be brought to fear *her* as well.

"Sassy girl," she murmured in Prospero's ear. "Disobedient, *not* the sweet child she was once, cannot be governed, lusty, lusty. . . ."

Prospero raised his hand. "Go into the lodge, or I shall strike you!" he cried.

"Go, 'Randa." Caliban's voice was low. Prospero turned with his still-raised hand and with it struck the youth, who did not flinch. Caliban's eyes grew hard, and he clenched his fists. But he stood motionless, holding his anger.

"Stop it!" yelled Miranda through tears. "Papa!"

Prospero's frown loosened, and for a moment he looked at his hand as though it belonged to a stranger.

Quickly Ariel fanned the fantasies and the fears in his mind, and they leapt up like flame. He raised his head, again frowning fiercely, and darted his eyes from Miranda to Caliban. "You two are plotting against me, laughing at me behind my back. I *will* rule my house! I *will* protect my daughter from beasts of the wild!"

"Go," Caliban mouthed to Miranda. With a quick, tearful look at her friend, she went into the house.

Once she had disappeared, Caliban looked straight at Prospero. His eyes were still hard, but his words were humble. "I will cut you some wood if you wish it, master."

Prospero only glanced at him with a strange mix of hatred, confusion, and fear, and said, "There's wood enough within. Get into your hut, monster. And come not near my daughter again."

CHAPTER 13

The Tempest

The pebble landed on the hard dirt floor of the rude shed where Miranda knelt, her eyes squeezed shut, her hands clapped prayerfully together. She heard it bounce but kept her eyes closed and continued mouthing the words her father had taught her. *"Mea culpa, mea maxima culpa, mea culpa, mea maxima culpa . . ."*

"Hssst!"

She opened her eyes in time to flinch and recoil. The second pebble narrowly missed her nose. *"Go away!"* she whispered fiercely. "If he sees you, you'll be cooked!"

"And you, 'Randa?" Caliban said from the other side of the bamboo wall.

"I'm cooked already. He's making me pray to

the Virgin. He does that only when he's *very* angry."

"The Virgin? Who's that? And what *is* this place? He didn't ask me to help him with it, for a wonder. He can no more build than he can bake."

Miranda sighed her agreement. The shed was lopsided and lurching; it would blow down in the next hard rain.

"Another one of *those*?" Caliban poked a finger between two bamboo rods to point at the rough wooden cross, tied with a twisted vine, that hung from the wall before Miranda. "Isn't the one in your lodge enough for him?"

"No! This is a church. He says he should have built it when he first landed on the island. He beats his head and says it is very wrong that among all his books he neglected to bring a Bible."

"A what?"

"*I* don't know!" Miranda whispered urgently, turning her head and abandoning her prayerful posture. "But go! He'll beat you."

"Meet me in an hour at the bird rocks. The big boulder, nearest the wood, fifty paces from the quicksand marsh."

"I do not know if I can steal away in an hour. I

must sit and recount to him the lives of virtuous women."

"I'll wait there. I have done my day's work, and the sight of me displeases him."

Caliban limped stealthily away moments before Prospero poked his head out of the lodge, frowning and holding a thick, crumbling book.

Hovering above the badly built shed, Ariel frowned. Invisibly she winged after Caliban to the wave-splashed rocks.

Caliban sat for hours at the start of the bird rocks, a jetty of boulders that began behind a screen of palms and ran into the sea from the cove's north-east curve. At the jetty's end waves crashed loudly and shot their salt spray twelve feet into the air.

Ariel perched nearby on the branch of a scrubby pine, wearing the form of a sleepy owl with one closed eye. With the open eye, she watched him.

She was still watching when Miranda came to him after supper (finch's eggs, flying fish, and hearts of palm, which Caliban had gathered and not been invited to eat).

"I said I was going for a bath in the salt pond," Miranda said, laughing a little sadly. She handed

Caliban a fried fish, which he chewed hungrily. "My father watches me like a gull now and will be searching for me within this half hour. But right now some book has seized him, and he only said, 'Hum.'"

"May lobsters gnaw his brains," grumbled Caliban as he swallowed the last of the fish and hurled a pebble into the sea. "I was slave enough to him before. Now he treats me worse than a dog, and I will not long endure it."

"Patience," Miranda said soothingly. "You have seen his fits in the past. And what do you know of dogs? *I've* never seen one. There are none on the island."

"There are. Wild ones. I have seen their shades run on the mountain by moonlight and heard them baying. Villainous things are they, and their howls chill my blood. They've grown louder this week."

Ariel knew that what Caliban had really seen and heard were her, Acrazia, Nous, and Fantasia on their midnight romps through the island's high rocks. And why not? They could be dogs when they pleased. She could do whatever she would.

Never had her confidence been so great, or her desire to conquer the island so strong. And then there was Prospero's dukedom across the sea, to be shared by the two of them, though she of course would have the upper hand. And perhaps *other* islands would fall under her sway, after this one had been won. There were so many worlds to conquer!

Meanwhile, she would trumpet her presence right here, near her cove, and bark like a wild dog with her minions whenever she wanted to. Next time, she determined, they would howl louder still.

Caliban and Miranda had fallen silent as Ariel mused. She could see little of their minds, since Miranda's was guarded from her by Prospero's feared command and Caliban's by his own hatred and mistrust of her. She could only sense their vague unease regarding this new anger of Prospero's, concerning them. Despite Miranda's comforting words, both knew this new wrath was much more serious than his other dark moods had been. Usually his broodings were brief. But his recent rage surpassed all his prior testy outbursts, and though it had now been a week since he'd surprised Miranda and Caliban in the clearing, his brow had not cleared.

"This morning I heard him muttering about someone named Althea," Caliban said. "'She was a piece of virtue!' he said. 'But *Miranda*!'"

Miranda sighed. "Yes. Althea was my mother. He never used to speak of her to me. Now he does, but says no more but that she was better than I am."

"Yesterday he beat me for not covering myself with a garment when I chopped wood. What madness! It is August now, and it was midday, and the air was hot as fire!"

Miranda smiled. "I like to watch you chop," she said sweetly.

He looked at her guardedly. "You must be melting under there!" He pulled at the clumsily spun wool cape Miranda had been wearing for a week. It hooded her and shrouded her entire body from neck to knees. Impatiently, she untied it and cast it aside on the warm rocks. She shook her hair out over her bare shoulders. Red-brown, it fell past her tight chest sheath of woven banana leaves, brushing the midpoint of her lower back. She smiled at him again.

Now his look was regretful. "He will kill me if I touch you."

"He could not kill you," she said with a troubled frown. "You are the stronger."

"But I do not wish to injure him," Caliban said reluctantly.

"Only that lobsters may gnaw his brains?" she teased.

Caliban grimaced. "Well, he angers me. But he's been like a father to me in the past, or like I think a father might be. Perhaps he will recover from what ails him now."

Miranda stayed silent, rubbing her toe in the sand. At length she said, "I don't wish you to harm him either. But I do not think he will recover from . . . what ails him now."

"Why?"

Miranda's face darkened with anger. "Some sickness has come over him. I am ashamed to tell you what he says."

"Tell me!"

She looked at him, her face mottled by her blush. "He forbids me your company because . . ."

"Because *what*?"

"He has been reading another book now, by a Greek sage named Ariss-Tottle. He reads and nods and reads and nods. He says the book proves what should be clear to any fool."

"Which is *what*?"

"That you and I are not of the same species!" she blurted.

Caliban frowned in puzzlement. "And this means what?"

"It is senseless. He is crazed, Caliban. He says

you are a 'freckled whelp, hag-born.' I said you were no such thing, and that's when he sent me to pray to the Virgin."

"He called me a *what? You* have more freckles than I do!"

"That is true." Miranda glanced at her own pink-brown arms and then at Caliban's arms, which were smooth and chocolatey. She reached to touch his wrist, but he drew back. She dropped her hand into her lap. "Well. He says that . . ." Her face grew still more crimson, but she met his eyes. "That I am human, while you are an island oddity, a sort of . . ." Her voice faded into silence, and she looked out at the ocean. The waves crashed on the rocks below them.

Caliban stared at her in disbelief. Then he stood abruptly, or tried to stand, but his twisted leg threw him off-balance, and he fell. Angrily he pushed himself up. "So. When he calls me monster, he truly means it! Thinks I'll people the island with freaks."

Now Miranda looked at him sorrowfully. "*I* don't think you're a freak or a monster. Don't hate me because he's gone mad. Please believe me; I am pleading for you. Though that only makes things worse! This morning as you mended the nets, he locked me in the woodshed. There I was, hemmed in like a carpenter ant, while he preached through the door. He said others would soon come to the island, men of my own kind, and—"

"*Your* kind! Fools with fish-belly faces who can't even catch a trout with a spear!"

Miranda paled at the insult. "I can't help the color of my face. And I *did* get a sea bass."

"They're slower."

"What does it matter? He has forbidden me to fish with you now, and so you and I must—"

"And you obey him! You kneel and pray to that silly virgin goddess he doesn't even think me fit to be told about, and you talk to me only behind his back—"

"I am your friend! I have not betrayed you, but I cannot abandon my father! Can't you see that whatever has gripped him makes him suffer too? He mutters, and his head aches so!" She stood and grabbed Caliban's elbow.

Again he shook off her hands. "Easy to suffer from headache while you lie in the hammock and let a monster-man mend your fishing line," he said bitterly.

She clapped her palms together, addressing him prayerfully, as though he himself were the invisible god in her father's new bamboo church. "Caliban, counsel me. I don't know what to do! It is dangerous to defy him openly. In his madness he may do great harm. I can still remember the great flame that nearly ruined the island, the first night of our sojourn here. I was but a child, but it still burns in my mind. It scarred your back. And every day since, we have seen him light the cook fire with a flick of his hand!"

"And we have also seen that those magical fires don't cook anything. I stuck my hand in one once; they don't even really burn! You don't fear him, you—" He avoided her pleading eyes and howled, "You agree with him!"

"No!" She reached for him again, but he was already moving quickly down the rocks, faster than she could follow. Tears filled her eyes and made his image double, then triple, a reflection in troubled water. She blinked, squinted, and saw him single again, and alone, a dark form dropping to the white beach.

She admired his muscular arms.

Yet her father's words came into her mind and troubled her. "Lurching monster," Prospero had said. "Freakish." Furious at herself, she shook her head, trying to empty it of the slanders.

But her father's words stayed. They floated beneath her thoughts' surface, as dark and as slimy as seaweed.

Caliban dove into the waves, his black hair streaming behind him. His heaviness melted into grace as he swam from view, around the curve of the island.

When he pulled himself to shore on the lesser rocks, he was crying. He was still wiping angry tears from his cheeks as he loped into the cool shade of the jungle. "He was *my* father too," he sobbed. "I'll kill him. Death to Prospero! The island should be mine!" He beat his brow with the heel of his hand. "Ah, *what* makes him hate me?"

Miranda still sat on the rocks, looking sad and confused. *What has changed everything?* she thought mournfully.

Above her, a sleepy-eyed owl on the jutting branch of a pine shook its wings suddenly and flew toward the clearing. After a few seconds it simply disappeared in the middle of the air.

"*That* was drama," Ariel shouted to her three minions as they sported in the surf at sunset, amid a pod of jumping dolphins. "I can make nothing of that ugly stick cross the duke built, and the virgin he makes his daughter pray to is too much like Setebos for my liking. But a bit of conflict is here, and I make so many interesting pictures fly through Prospero's head now! Dark monsters ravaging snowy princesses, freakish children calling him Grandpapa—these pictures don't please him as much as the others I've made, but I like them. And you silly ones do too, do you not?"

"Yesssss!" Nous shot up into the darkening sky, came down as three falling stars, and dropped into the ocean with a hiss. Acrazia took the form of a shimmering coral, while Fantasia joined a school of flying fish that skimmed the ocean's top. Ariel sat crowned above them in the air, wearing the handsome face and robes of a young pasha she had seen drawn with bright colors in one of her master's books. "Applaud for me, my minions!" she said exultantly. The three junior spirits grew hands that clapped, and throats that burst into song.

Caliban stayed deep in the forest now, while Miranda moped, and Prospero muttered to himself, after a few days of burned food, that perhaps he had been too hard on the monster.

"He is better off gone," Ariel sang to Prospero

at night. "Perhaps he has joined the cannibals on the far side of the island, the ones your soldiers will help us to conquer when the easterners arrive here, soon, soon. In the meantime, I will help you keep guard against all of them."

"Oh, you will, will you?" said Prospero, nervous and skeptical. He had heard drumming in his dreams for three nights running, had woken thrice with his heart pounding, and was not at all well rested. "You, airy spirit, will protect me from a hundred cannibals? I would be better pleased if you would chop some wood for the fire. There's none to do it since Caliban disappeared; my back is old, and I tire easily."

"I am sorry," Ariel sang cheerily. "I—"

He stopped her with a raised hand and a sigh. "I know. You were not made for that kind of work."

Miranda could chop and carry wood nearly as well as Caliban, but her father forbade her to do this and other arduous island tasks now. He insisted that she sit quietly, repairing their simple garments, praying to the Virgin, or listening to comportment lessons, which he said he should have begun years before. "*Don't* splay your legs like that when you sit, daughter!" he snapped. "And when you meet a young nobleman, you must curtsy and offer your hand for him to kiss." He took her hand in his and looked worriedly at its rough calluses. "Well . . . perhaps we might forgo the hand kissing. What matters the hand? Your soul holds virtues enough to charm any lord, dear daughter, if you would only come to your senses."

"Papa, what *nobleman* shall I meet on this island?" asked Miranda disgustedly, snatching her hand back. "There is no one here but you and me and Caliban, and not even Caliban now, since you have driven him away. . . ." Her voice trailed off. She remembered the last, hurt look Caliban had given her as they stood on the bird rocks, and knew it was not only her father who had driven her friend away. Perhaps she should have run after him and never returned to the clearing, with its roughly built shelters and its crude little church. Perhaps she should have lived with Caliban in the forest, or even journeyed with him to the other side of the island, leaving her father alone. But how could she have done such a thing? She had seen poor Prospero aging year after year, sitting by the fire with his books, turning their pages as though he might find some treasure in them to soothe his sadness. One night, when he'd thought she slept, she had even heard him weeping.

The sound had harrowed her heart. She herself could barely remember any place besides this island, and was happy here, but her father was an exile. Perhaps it was stark homesickness that was now unsettling his mind.

She set her face grimly. No, she could not leave him utterly alone. He needed her.

"I think a visit of noblemen to this shore is . . . unlikely, Papa," she said cautiously. "Now, as you said a moment ago, you might have been unfair to Cali—"

"Silence, girl!" Prospero said roughly. His eyes flashed fire. "I have a plan."

Behind him fluttered a pair of invisible wings.

Prospero shared his plan only with Ariel. Late at night, as they sat by the fire she made glow in rainbow colors, he rubbed his palms together, over and over, and she helped him plot. "It is good," he said, his eyes dark and wild. He pulled his beard. "Tempest and lightning and storm and humiliation for my brother, and oh, yes, the greatest revenge of all: not just that fiendish Antonio's death but the marriage of my daughter to the son of Alonso, king of Naples! For they all will be on board the vessel, and that young man cannot choose but love her."

"Not if you let me paint what he sees when he looks at her," Ariel sang.

Prospero looked briefly wounded at this suggestion that his daughter's beauty needed magical improvements. But he was too thrilled at the thought of impending revenge to argue. "Ah, Ariel, my chick," he gloated. "I will have my dukedom back, and Miranda will marry a prince, and my heirs will gain a greater kingdom than I have lost!"

"And we will conquer the rest of the island," Ariel reminded him.

"Oh, yes, yes, that we will," said Prospero absently.

Two weeks passed. Ariel let the island grow breeze-less and charged it with the tension and dread of Prospero's mind.

There came a day when the air went heavy and silent. No birds sang. The sun lay alone, a hot disk in the cloudless sky. Light sparkled and winked on the ridges of the blue waves, as though the water were sprinkled with magic dust from the shore's edge to the eastern horizon.

Prospero stood in his robe at the edge of the sea,

holding his gumbo-limbo–wood staff. About his head Ariel flew, invisible.

Miranda was fifteen that day, which was the Feast of Saint Bartholomew.

Prospero said, "It is time." He raised his staff. "They come."

Ariel turned the sky black.

Forth went her three spirits as lightning and hail-stones and rain, and she herself sailed far, far, many leagues out to sea, to the very rim of the Triangle. There, with all the strength she had gained in the years Prospero had listened to her, believed her tales, smiled at her music, given her life, she reached out-ward, outward, pushing the storm-filled Triangle far-ther, farther, farther, a thousand leagues farther out into the Atlantic. . . .

It caught the lone wooden ship that had blown off its course and lost a sail and for weeks run west-ward with the wind. Ariel pulled the vessel with its terrified sailors into the Triangle.

"Save us!" they shrieked, and she laughed.

For these mariners the magic shape was no refuge from a storm outside, as it had been for Sycorax and, centuries before, for Jasper. Now the Triangle was a terrifying province of tempest that mercilessly sucked, drawing them from calmer seas and tossing them until they vomited and screamed and prayed. Only the captain kept his head. He climbed into the rigging and tried to control the ropes and the remaining sails. But Ariel ripped the sheets ragged and blew the mast down, flaming amazement, burning on the bowsprit and the topsail and the deck, until men jumped screaming into the boiling water, led by a youth with curled chestnut hair who cried, "Hell is empty, and all the devils are here!"

Ariel drove the ship and its men onward, leagues onward, toward the island, and finally into a smaller cove on the isle's southeastern side. While the storm still raged, she put the sailors to sleep on the deck of the boat. Prospero had said, "We shall need them for our future journey."

The men who had jumped into the sea for fear, she blew through the waves and up on the beach. Prospero had said, "I will need them for my present revenge."

The youth with the curled hair, who had yelled and jumped first, she blew far from the others, making sails of his fancy balloon sleeves and his cape. She washed him into an odd angle of the island and left him sitting there with his fine locks bedraggled and his arms folded in a sad knot, his teeth chattering and his lips blue. Prospero had said, "I will need him for Miranda."

When all this playful work was done, Ariel dove into the ground before Prospero, who still stood at the edge of the water, laughing madly and yelling in wordless triumph, his hair blowing wildly, his wooden staff raised as though the storm were his doing alone. She raced in sand circles around his feet like the fastest of snakes and shook inwardly with laughter.

CHAPTER 14

Revenge

The men sat in their water-stained silks, shivering and grumbling in the chill wind Ariel blew on them. She knew them by the names they called one another, and by the looks of them, and by the thoughts she could read in their minds.

Antonio was a beak-nosed fellow some years younger than his brother, Prospero. Ariel could see the bones of the duke's face in his. But looking into Antonio's eyes, she saw that he was, in all other ways, nothing like her master. His thoughts were full of facts, things like nautical miles and wind speeds and sums of money, and the questions he was asking himself were not what magic had blown them hither and what sort of story he was in, but whether the trunks containing his cash might just possibly have washed up on the island, as he had, and be sitting on the next beach. She doubted that he could be distracted from *his* troubles with an air vision of the marvelous siege of Troy.

Alonso, the king of Naples, looked to be about Prospero's age, though he was balder. He was another hard-minded man like Antonio, although a look at Alonso's mind told her he was not planning a search for lost money but was grieving, grieving, grieving. And since grief was a thing she could not understand, and because its presence in a human's mind made all of that mind's pictures dark and unclear, she did not know the substance of his thought until he spoke it aloud.

"Ferdinand!" he said with a sob. "Ah, sweet Ferdinand! Lost to the sea before your eighteenth birthday! And I had planned to buy you an ermine robe, and a horse of Araby, and a pound of those special sweet sugar dates you love . . . the ones you got sick on last Easter—oh, oh!" He buried his face in his knees.

Ariel turned a somersault in the air, laughing silently. She knew that Alonso's beloved chestnut-haired Ferdinand was himself clutching his knees on a beach less than half a league distant, sobbing for the loss of his papa and—no doubt—of the promised birthday presents. Their tears would not soften her. These men who sat before her now, including Alonso, were her master's enemies, and their punishment would rival Achilles' vengeance against Hector.

She narrowed her eyes and heard battle cries, saw phantom spears flashing in the sun. With her at his side, she saw Prospero sitting in air, crowned with diamonds, and raising a great sword above the neck of his brother, Antonio, who knelt humbly on the ground before him, with head bowed. Singing a triumphant, rhyming ballad of revenge, Prospero smote Antonio, and his head fell off. In her vision Ariel, eyes blazing and purple, held the head aloft and cried, "Prospero shall be king! March we to the far side of the island!" And a roar rose from the throats of the watching army, who wore horsehair-ridged helmets like those of the Greeks.

Marvelous scene! Ariel thought. Were it to go well in performance, she saw no reason why it might not be played a second time, or even a third, with variations. Antonio's head might be rejoined to his neck, then lopped off again by Prospero—to a different vengeful song, perhaps, for which she would compose new music—and this time bounced about like a ball on the beach or knocked with a bone. That thought reminded her of old Jasper's bones, the hardiest of which still poked from the sand on the far side of the cove, so brittle now it would have crumbled into powder had she used it to bat a ball or beat a drum. She cared nothing for that bone, which to her only suggested that its original owner had cast it aside along with the rest of his body when he flew to some other island.

Perhaps these men who sat shivering before her now could someday supply new bones for play.

She heard a cough and turned to meet the eyes of a third man, dressed more humbly than the other two in woolen leggings and a plain canvas shirt. He made a gesture as though to doff a cap but found that whatever hat had topped his head had washed away in the water. "My master," he said plaintively.

"Ah, what is it, Gonzalo?" snapped Alonso, raising his head with a look of vexation.

Old Gonzalo bowed. "Forgive me, master, but I would counsel you not to despair of your son. We washed up on this beach by some sort of magic. Why might not Ferdinand have done the same? And what a fine place this is! Why, it looks to me as if honeydew and grapes and ambrosia, the very nectar of the gods, grew here, just beyond this very cove!" He spread his arms vaguely and wide.

Antonio and Alonso looked dubiously about them. The particular patch of beach where Ariel had stranded them was in fact a very scrubby one, dotted with stunted logwood trees rather than the stately palms of her own cove, and the sand was coarse.

She cawed like a crow above their heads. Gonzalo cupped his ear. "Ah! The bird of paradise! Let us rise and explore, my masters! I doubt not that we shall find not only the lost Ferdinand but the fountain of eternal youth in this island, along with emeralds and topazes and rubies as big as our heads, lying about for the gathering—nay, growing on trees!"

Antonio rolled his eyes. He said, "I will satisfy myself with a search for our strongbox. It held fifty pounds of silver, as well as the gold that was given for Princess Claribel. No doubt the box sits at the bottom of the ocean, but I cling to a spar of hope. Perhaps the waves pushed it to shore. I will make sure before I despair of it."

"Emeralds and rubies and topazes and the fountain

of youth!" Gonzalo exulted, his arms in the air and his eyes squeezed shut.

Ariel danced invisibly in the sky. Gonzalo's mind would have made her mouth water had she been possessed of a tongue. She itched to enter it.

Prospero had spoken well of this man, Gonzalo. "An old servant, who was good to me," he'd said. "He could not disobey the king and my brother's command that I be put out to sea, but he made sure I was supplied with a little food and with my precious books. Be gentle with him, Ariel." And so she would be. She would just give Gonzalo more of the fancies on which he now floated. What sport it would be!

Yet that sport would have to wait. For she had now an even more delicious task in hand.

She flew.

"Full fathom five."

The youth raised his head and wiped his nose with a fine lace sleeve. That nose was well formed, as sharp as a pen, and his cheeks were the rosy hue of a salmon's belly.

Ariel sang again, in the voice of an angel.

167

> *"Full fathom five thy father lies;*
> *Of his bones are coral made;*
> *Those are pearls that were his eyes:*
> *Nothing of him that doth fade*
> *But doth suffer a sea-change*
> *Into something rich and strange."*

The youth had stopped crying at the third note of her music. "Is this isle magical?" His voice held wonder. "Who sings? Your song gives me hope that I am not alone. Is it possible?"

She saw the tide of his black grief ebbing.

She knew she could lead him now.

He followed her musical voice to the clearing, and there, in the shade of the trees, he stopped short.

Prospero crouched by the hut. At his first sight of the pale youth, he started and looked dubious, as though a sudden memory had told him his plan might not, after all, be the best one. Ariel raced to him and kissed his ear. "Dear master, it works!" she whispered. "What a glorious young man, and *so* wealthy! He will make your daughter a queen!"

"Ye-e-e-e-sss," Prospero said, still looking slightly troubled. But Ariel kissed him again, and he stayed where he was, watching the lad intently.

In the center of the clearing sat Miranda, humming and washing berries in a bucket of springwater. At her father's mysterious command, she had clothed herself in garments of deerskin she had pounded with sand days before and laid in the sun until they bleached almost white. Now they shone against her red-brown skin.

She looked well enough. She was square faced, of course, and her nose was blunt. Her form was muscular and solid and a little bit plump. But as Ariel danced before Ferdinand's eyes, throwing clouds into them, she grew to him as slender as a reed, and her skin blanched and became as lily-white as the skin of certain Neapolitan ladies he had been told were the loveliest of their kind. Her green eyes shone like the emeralds old Gonzalo hoped to find growing on the island's palm trees.

"The wonder of her!" Ferdinand breathed. "Loveliest of lovelies!"

"Things go well, great duke," Ariel whispered.

Had she had a heart, it would have trembled. The task she had craved for years lay before her now, and she awaited only her master's command to unleash her powers.

He hesitated a moment. "He was a spoiled and whining child," he murmured. "Always stuffing himself with sugarsops and waited on hand and foot. Ah, the poor girl, if he has not grown manlier . . ."

"He *has*!" Ariel hissed. "Do not think on it! Things go well!" She kissed him a third time.

His face hardened. "Then you may go to her, my love," he said, his voice grim and purposeful. "Now, I lift my ban."

Within a split second Ariel was at Miranda's shoulder.

Ferdinand walked, as if in a trance, into the open space of the clearing. His garments were torn, and the skin on his smooth, straight limbs was visible through the rents. Stiffened by salt, his thick chestnut hair stood up straight, like the quills of a porcupine. His wide-set eyes shone with dreams. He rubbed his nose absently and stepped on a branch, which broke with a crack.

Miranda looked up at him as Ariel spread her wings over her head. The girl's green eyes widened. She stood, spilling her berries to the ground.

She was at sea, her mind tossed by tempest. With her deepest thought she heard Caliban's voice calling her from the forest, and she fought to answer him, to cry out to him, to remember him. But a new force like a hand pushed her down, and she was drowning. Like a wave, the strange power caught her up, turned her around, and sent her crashing. She could think nothing for herself, and her eyes were blurred with water. All she could see was this creature who now stood before her, this youth who seemed unlike anyone she'd known outside a dream.

In a voice full of awe she asked Ferdinand, "Are you a god?"

"Keep fanning," Prospero whispered, crouched by the hut. "Yes, yes, good! All's well! She likes him! Keep fanning."

Ariel hovered a foot from Ferdinand's face, quickly beating her purple gossamer wings so that a perfumed breeze blew directly into the young man's eyes. Then she rose, flew close to Miranda, and repeated the action. The hair of the lovers blew back from their faces as though pushed by a soft island breeze. They could not see Ariel or her wings, could see only each other.

Ferdinand fell to his knees before Miranda. "Oh, let me worship *you*, fair mistress!" he crooned. "Come live with me and be my love!"

"Wife," murmured Prospero through clenched

teeth, in a voice only Ariel could hear. "Wife!"

Ariel flew over Ferdinand's head and beat her wings harder.

"I shall marry you!" Ferdinand sang, raising his hands skyward in exultation, as Miranda blushed and giggled. Deep inside her, a trapped, drowning part of her heart listened in shock to that giggle.

Ferdinand clapped his palms together. "If my father will only agree . . . but wait! He's dead! I myself am lord of all he possessed, and that was much! Great estates in Italy, and you shall be the queen of them!"

"Very good!" whispered Prospero fiercely. "Yes, very good!"

Ariel flew to Miranda and brushed her eyes with her wings, making the girl blink. Then she flew back to Ferdinand. In Miranda's eyes Ferdinand's pale, pampered handsomeness grew into something indefinably glorious. The girl thought she saw a crown or a halo hovering above his brow (a mirage produced by Ariel, who was now circling Ferdinand's head as fast as any hummingbird).

While her buried heart groaned, all the bold speech and loud laughter Miranda had shared with Caliban melted into shyness and blushes. Now she was truly submerged in a strange magic. She felt horrified, but when she looked into Ferdinand's worshipful eyes, she also felt a strange, tingling pleasure. She was sea-changed, not herself, a leaf awash in a current. Her actions, her words, and even her thoughts were like those of a dreamer, or an actor in a play.

She cast her eyes to the ground and simpered, "I am yours if you think me worthy, brave prince!"

"Now is my part," Prospero whispered, and advanced toward the pair. Ariel had lent him flashing eyes and brightened the colors of his cloak. He wore a necklace of cowrie shells, and his hair stood up like horns on his head. Ferdinand looked up at him in fear and opened his mouth to speak, but Prospero raised his gumbo-limbo staff and roared, "*Silence!* I am the ruler of this island and the master of this fair maid! Only I have the power to grant her to you!"

Ferdinand was already on his knees. Now he fell prostrate on the earth before Prospero, groveling, further muddying his already soiled silks. "Ah, great magician, I know not who you are, or from whence you and your daughter come. But surely you too are at least half divine, and I will perform your every command if only you will grant me this perfect maiden for my wife!"

"I require that statement in writing." From a sleeve of his robe Prospero produced a scroll of banana leaves, crudely stitched together. "In my, er, island palace"—he gestured toward his lodge, which Ariel, flying over it, caused to look like a Roman villa—"is a gull-feather pen and berry ink. The document awaits you."

"I will sign anything!" Ferdinand rose to his knees and made as if to stand. Prospero pointed his staff at him, and Ariel sat on Ferdinand's shoulders. The young man fell forward on his hands, while Miranda watched in amazement.

"First let me warn you that its first article commits you not to touch her before the wedding, and its second to stock my woodpile!" Prospero barked.

Ferdinand looked doubtful for a moment. "But I have never . . . Have you no servants to do such—"

Ariel jumped up and down on his back, and he fell prostrate in the dust once more. "I shall carry wood!" he yelled.

"Hmm, hmm," Prospero muttered worriedly as he hastened with Ariel toward the cove where she'd left the other men. "Will this hold? I wonder. The boy is courteous enough, but can he *truly* make her happy?

Your magic is strong, Ariel, but can it last both their lifetimes? Althea and I had troubles enough. . . . Though once the youngsters are fast married, they'll have to make do, I suppose. . . . And our family's wealth will be increased, that's good, that's . . . *more* than good, it's excellent. But ah, the unwelcome memories the sight of Ferdinand brought back! He *was* a peevish child. How could I have forgotten the time he drank my paints, thinking they were sweet berry juice, and then was sick on the floor, all over my manuscripts! And of course *I* was blamed by his father for leaving the paints about. But who had asked the brat into my study? Foolish of Althea, always leaving the door open when she came in to dust, as though my private place were like any other room in the house!"

He was veering into the kinds of thoughts Ariel could not understand and which bored her. Images of household accounts and loud-voiced marital squabbles and whining children plodded through his brain, and she blew into his ear, turning them into dust. She replaced them with pictures of a blazing sword and of treacherous heads bouncing on the beach, all in syncopated rhythm. "Think of your revenge on your brother!"

"Ah, yes," he said, brightening a little. "My revenge!"

The three stranded men had gone exploring, looking for the strongbox, and were now resting near the quicksand swamp, half a league from where Ariel had first washed them ashore. She found them by following the fevered dreams of carbuncles and emeralds and rubies in Gonzalo's mind, which were so strong they had left a visible trail in the air.

The men were footsore and had not found their money, and she had sent Acrazia, Nous, and Fantasia as an invisible cloud of flies to plague Alonso and Antonio. Now they twisted and fidgeted amid the vine-laden trees, slapping bugs they could not see. Their moods were foul. Only Gonzalo, buoyed up by his visions, still smiled.

"Just beyond that next tree, I warrant we will find our treasures!" he crowed, gesturing in the direction of the quicksand. "I hear sweet music, I smell sweet perfumes!"

"Shut your wine hole, you old fool," Antonio growled. He was dancing about in a frenzy, his back to Prospero, who crouched with Ariel, tensely watching, behind a mahogany tree. "Can't you help us fight these man-eating insects?"

"They plague me not," said Gonzalo placidly. "I say, let us build a city on this island—"

"No doubt they plague you not because your dry old flesh tastes like leather!" Antonio snapped. "But you could help us beat them off, all the same!"

Gonzalo came toward him and halfheartedly waved his hand at the invisible swarm of sprite insects. His eyes were crammed with dreams. "Governor Gonzalo . . ." he murmured. "Governor Gonzalo . . ."

Prospero covered his mouth and laughed heartily with Ariel.

Alonso was not railing at Gonzalo but moaning softly as he tried to wave off the sprite flies. He turned his head, and when Prospero saw his tears, his laughter ceased.

"He is dead," Alonso wept. "My only son is drowned."

At that moment Antonio turned, and Prospero saw his brother's face.

"My God," he said softly. "Oh, my brother— Antonio!" Impulsively, he stepped forward.

"Stop!" Ariel hissed, pulling at his robe. "Would you spoil all? Your brave plot!"

"Yes, yes, of course." Prospero stepped back uncertainly. "It is just that . . . he looks so old!" He touched his beard and muttered, "Am *I* so old?"

He took another step back into invisibility. The leaves under his foot crunched, and Antonio paused in his anguished fly swatting to look around suddenly, frowning. "What was that?"

"My son!" Alonso said hopefully, and the three men rushed to the edge of the clearing. Ariel hid Prospero with her wings, and the men saw nothing.

"He is not here," Antonio said, clapping Alonso's shoulder in sympathy. "Some island animal, it must have been. I fear you were right. We must think Ferdinand drowned and not delude ourselves with false hopes."

Alonso's despair looked greater than before, and he burst into new tears. Antonio patted his shoulder.

"Dispense with the flies," Prospero hissed to Ariel.

Ariel looked at him in bafflement, but blinked, and her three buzzing sprites melted away. So preoccupied was Alonso with his mourning, and Antonio with Alonso's collapse, that the men took a moment to notice that the sprites had stopped biting.

"Ah, they're gone," Antonio said with satisfaction.

"Now, friends, let's look for some food."

"I doubt not that this island contains great delicacies for our eating pleasure!" Gonzalo said hopefully.

Without waiting for Prospero's command, Ariel caused a banquet table to hover in the air before them. It was loaded with roast boar, sweetmeats, and wine in gold flagons. Looking stunned, Gonzalo and Antonio reached for the table. Ariel clapped her wings and made it all disappear.

"Ah!" said Gonzalo in disappointment.

"A mirage." Antonio's voice was matter-of-fact. "Sprung from our hunger and thirst and our longing."

Alonso had barely marked the illusory table. His weeping grew louder.

"See, master?" Ariel said gleefully. "Look at them! In very ill humor. Your revenge works, and the best part is yet to come! Were I human, I would pity them!"

Prospero looked at her strangely. The frown he'd worn when they left Miranda and Ferdinand in the clearing had returned to his brow. His eyes looked piercingly into hers, which were limpid and more purple than ever before. "But you are *not* human," he said.

She looked at him in puzzlement.

"Well," he said shortly, "I have had enough of this. Somehow it happens not as I imagined it would, or perhaps it is just that I am not enjoying it as much as I thought I would. Not any of it—not my daughter's meeting with young Ferdinand, not my foes' distress. But the play must be played out. We will continue. Say the piece we wrote together. Poetry will put things in order. It always has."

"Yes, yes, yes, master!" Ariel clapped her hands. "The speech of vengeance!"

She swelled and grew wings the size of whale flukes and the head of a lion. She flew into the center of the clearing and made herself visible at last. Gonzalo fell on his knees before her, his hands shielding his face.

She roared.

"You three
From Milan did supplant good Prospero,
Expos'd unto the sea,
Him and his innocent child: for which foul deed
The powers, delaying, not forgetting, have
Incensed the seas and shores, yea, all the creatures,
Against your peace. Thee of thy son, Alonso,

They have bereft; and do pronounce by me:
Lingering perdition, worse than any death
Shall step by step attend you and your ways.
Unless the king repent, and you, Antonio—"

Antonio drew his sword and waved it in the air. It sliced through Ariel, leaving her as before, and she laughed. *"Quiver with fear, and then prepare for doom!"* she bellowed, and vanished.

"More illusion," Antonio said, sheathing his sword. "Gnats buzzing. Though something in their buzzing reminded me of my poor lost brother, Prospero, and his stupid sailboat. Remember? Ah, how Althea still mourns him! Sailing from Lisbon, scanting work, with a baby girl stowed in the prow, to be lessoned, no doubt, in Greek poetry! Sheer folly! And overloaded with books, as usual."

Prospero stiffened behind his tree. *"What?"* he whispered.

Antonio glared at Gonzalo. "You should have stopped him, old fellow, not bade him good journey and loaded more books in!"

Gonzalo ignored him. He was still staring, open-mouthed, at the spot in the air where Ariel had been. "Now I *know* this isle is filled with glories!" he said.

"Phoenixes and unicorns too, no doubt! We will catch them, we will be famous. . . ."

Alonso too was not listening to Antonio. He had thrown himself on the ground in a fit of grief. "Idiot, idiot!" he was wailing. "The very voices in the air condemn me! Why did I indulge Ferdinand's squeamish vanity? He wouldn't even learn to swim, said that skill was for common fishermen! And now he's drowned, drowned. . . ."

"Ariel!" Prospero barked in a fierce whisper.

She shot to her master's side. "Now you may chop off Antonio's head!" she said excitedly.

"Don't be foolish. I have no sword!"

She blinked, and a jeweled dagger shimmered in the air before him.

"Foolishness, Ariel, foolishness! That's as airy as your banquet! Come with me. Leave them to their grief awhile. We'll return to them anon. . . . Must do that, else they may wander into some sticky dangers. But first I must . . . I am remembering something . . . I must think. . . ."

Ariel pouted, and Prospero frowned deeply at her. "Come!"

He began to walk slowly back toward his clearing, while she flew sullenly behind him. In the trees to their rear, Gonzalo scraped in the ground for jewels, while Antonio urged Alonso to rise and walk, to look for Ferdinand, if he would, or at least for fresh water.

CHAPTER 15

Prospero Wakes

"Sit there," Prospero told Ariel, who hovered near his shoulder. She had taken on a girl's face and wavy blue-green seaweed hair and the form of a winged water nymph. He gestured toward a rock some five feet from him and looked at her nervously. "I would have you farther off."

She frowned and shrank a little bit in size, but complied. "What is it, master?" she said. "All goes well!"

"I am not so sure."

From his wooden stool behind the lodge Prospero regarded Ferdinand, who had collapsed under a weight of firewood that Caliban could have carried in one arm. He was moaning, as Miranda knelt, cooing, to stroke his forehead. "Dear Prince

Ferdinand, you were not meant for such lowly labor!" she said.

"Quite right," Ferdinand gasped, as he struggled to his feet. "But for you, my goddess . . ." He feebly reached for a stick of wood, but Miranda had already picked up the entire load and was bearing it easily into the lodge on her broad shoulders. Ferdinand called halfheartedly after her, "Ah, do not disgrace your divinity with this base task!"

Prospero sighed. "I may have been wrong about . . . some things," he said in a low voice. "Now that I see all their faces . . . Yes . . . I begin to think I have misjudged him."

Ariel peered at him in puzzlement. His mind was clouding again, throwing up that tiresome wall that kept her from playing with his thoughts, and she could not tell which "him" he meant. Perhaps he meant more than one. But why was he delaying their glorious revenge? She would write a song of it afterward, they would sing it together, and she would stage it in the air—

"To dream used to bring me such pleasure," Prospero said quietly. "It freed me from—all sorts of things—but now . . . so much lost by it! First my brother, next my young island friend, and finally my *daughter*—brave little Miranda, I hear nothing of your merry voice in that 'Dear Prince Ferdinand!'" Prospero mocked his daughter's simper, looking pained.

Ariel beat her wings furiously. "You should rest now, master," she sang in a low, soothing voice. "Sleep will restore you. Perchance you should dream. You are not well."

"No, I am *not* well," Prospero said. "I have not been well for quite some time. I have a tale to tell you, dearest of friends." He looked at her with sorrowful eyes.

She clapped her hands. "A story!"

"Yes. This one is true."

Her wings wilted slightly. "Oh," she said flatly. "But is it a *good* story?"

He shrugged impatiently. Then he placed his staff athwart his knees, leaned his elbows on it, and propped his chin on his hands. "I had forgotten this story, or much of it, in my years on this island, in your company." He looked at her sidelong. "Stay there, will you? It comes back to me, now. So strange. . . . Listen well.

"Many years ago in Milan lived a farmer. His father had left him a vineyard and a herd of cattle.

He'd a younger brother who was good at accounts, who worked tirelessly on the land, and who never ceased to pester the farmer with ideas . . . about improving the grapes, about rebuilding the barns, about joining with the richest landowner in Milan in a cattle-breeding experiment, to produce the finest livestock in Italy!"

Ariel began to snore. Prospero tried to rap her head smartly with his staff but failed. The wood met only air. "Listen, spirit!" he chided. "None of these notions did the farmer heed. His farm did not interest him. He wished, do you see . . ." Prospero laughed shamefacedly and shook his head. "He wished to be a poet. He ignored his farm and spent his time reading and writing. He squandered the harvest money on manuscripts, which he bought from the archbishop. He collected them: Greek romances, Roman mythology, travelers' tales, ballads in country dialects, a little philosophy; though, in truth, he preferred what rhymed. And oh, the places he would sail to in his head!" Prospero clutched his staff, and his eyes took on a soft, dreamy look. "To Troy with King Agamemnon, and to the fabled island of Lemnos with Jason and Hercules, or to the lost city of Atlantis. He was an Arab chieftain, racing his steed across shining hot sands, or a Viking warrior, riding the white crests of the icy waves! Or Odysseus, on the magical isle of the gorgeous nymph Calypso, who looked at him with violet eyes and called him her darling, forever. Ah, yes! All time was forgotten as he wandered in the lands of his dreams.

"But then a book would end, and he would shake his cloudy head and look out the window to see the weeds that had grown in the vineyard while he read, and would hear his hired men quarreling. Then his wife would stick her head into his room, with a squalling baby on her hip and a tired face—no Calypso she! She would bark at him, such tedious things: pay the men, see to the accounts! And his brother would come in from the fields, complaining about the weather, and his face, which before had looked merely irritable in a brotherly sort of way, would seem horrid and fiendish, like that of Odysseus's Cyclops or the three-headed dog who guards the gates of Hell!

"And so the man would close his books, sighing, and spend a little time on his accounts and see to the weeding. But at night he would go back to his poetry. In time he began to write long poems of his own, and to read them aloud, and circulate them among the townspeople. They were good poems, some of them—"

"Say them to me," begged Ariel.

Prospero shook his head. "This is not the time, brave spirit. Only listen. In time this man's farm began to fail, and his wife and brother railed at him more loudly than before. One day his brother went off without his permission and struck a deal with that rich Milanese landowner, a man born in Naples, who had grand holdings all over Italy. That man was called Alonso, and he had a whining, pesky little silk-clad son. . . ." Prospero glanced at Ferdinand, who was now resting on a fallen log on the far side of the clearing, while Miranda fed him strawberries. He sighed. "Well. The two men began to breed cattle together. And the cattle were fat and handsome and brought in money. And it was not long before the folk of Milan began to treat the farmer's young brother as though he were the—"

"Duke?" asked Ariel brightly. She rose and began to flutter toward Prospero, but he stopped her with an upraised hand.

"Are you listening?" he said in vexation. "Only *sit*. There are no dukes in Milan, not really! 'Duke' has a fine sound, but in fact the city is ruled by an archbishop. So duke me no duke! As I was saying, the people of Milan began to treat the brother as though he were truly the owner of the land, though in fact it belonged to . . . me. To me."

Prospero brooded for a moment, while Ariel sat blinking, hoping the story might take an exciting turn, and preparing some twists of her own to suggest in case it did not.

"Yes, well," Prospero said suddenly. "I have a tendency to be long-winded. Let me say simply that I went along with my brother, Antonio, grudgingly, because he was . . . well, he was right, I suppose, in everything; he and Alonso were making the farm a great success. Twelve years ago I even went so far as to accompany them to a great fair in Lisbon, held every four years and ending just before Saint Bartholomew's Day. There prizes are given, and cattle are sold, and fortunes can be greatly increased. I went unwillingly, because I was deep in the middle of an epic poem I was composing, about the destruction of the great empire of Atlantis—no, sit still, I will not recite it to you; you have heard it many times! Off to Lisbon we sailed, and once we got there, Antonio and Alonso were depending on me to help show our cattle and sell our wines, but such busi- ness was far too tedious for me to endure, and the water near the port looked inviting, so I sent my wife to help them instead, while I borrowed a boat and set sail with our daughter—poor Miranda! a week short of three years old!—for an afternoon of dreamy con- templation and poetry. I brought my oils, thinking I might paint a sunset. Though the paints washed over- board. I told my plan only to Alonso's servant, Gonzalo, who thought it a wonderful idea and packed us a dinner." He frowned as if in pain. "Of course I didn't tell Althea we were going boating— Ah, her grief! And to think she has mourned all these years! She would never have permitted my going. But I, fool that I am, sailed out into the bay, and the storm came up, and . . ." He let his voice trail off.

Ariel was looking at him brightly. Her eyes had turned a deep shade of purple, and in them he saw his own reflection, wearing a crown.

He averted his gaze from her face. After a moment he said, "All that I have just told you, you already knew."

She blinked at him and yawned a delicate yawn. "It's dull."

His fit of anger was on him suddenly, like a

squall. He threw his staff to the ground. "Yes, real life is commonplace, is it not?" he barked, rising. Startled, she quailed before him. "And you'll have no traffic with what's commonplace. Only extraordinary stories, fine tales, inventions, *lies*—" He turned from her and beat at his brow. "Oh, Prospero, Prospero . . . Oh, my head . . ."

"Father?" Miranda called to him from the far side of the clearing, where she and Ferdinand were gazing at him in alarm. "Are you well? To whom do you speak?"

Prospero dropped his hands quickly to his sides. "'Tis nothing." He summoned a ghost of his earlier commanding voice. "Ferdinand, arise! Get back to work!"

The youth pulled himself to his feet. "Yes, great magician!" His voice held a trace of reluctance.

"Shall I return to them?" said Ariel eagerly. "Shall I freshen his eyes and his ardor?"

Prospero looked at her in silence for a moment as she batted her wings. Then he said sadly, "You understand nothing of what I have said."

Ariel rose in the air and widened her gorgeous eyes. He looked into them longingly, then turned away with an effort, shielding his own. "What would you say to me, Ariel?" He kept his gaze on the ground.

"I say it is time for your great revenge! I have it well plotted!" Ariel's wings beat furiously. "Let us construct a hollow wooden horse, and wheel it onto the beach, and hide inside it! When they come to stare at it, we shall jump out of its belly and lop off their heads! Then I shall awaken the sailors who now sleep in the far cove, and they will honor you as a god, and we will march forward, chanting, to conquer the whole of the island!" Ariel burst into battle song, and Prospero covered his ears.

"Enough!" he whispered, as loudly as he could without attracting his daughter's attention again. "*Enough!* There is something eternally . . . *childish* about you! Murderous revenge was but a fantasy. I see that now. I will go to them in the woods where they wander, and—"

"No, master!" Ariel said. Prospero looked at her sharply, and she made her voice more submissive. "Master, you must rest now. You are confused. I will help you calm yourself. I will summon my minion spirits, and we will put on a fine show in the air! We will celebrate the betrothal of yon lovers."

Prospero looked dubiously at Ferdinand and

Miranda. The young man was again resting, his back against a tree, while Miranda straightened the cord of wood she had piled by the lodge.

"We spirits will appear as singing gods!" Ariel said sweetly.

"All right, Ariel," Prospero said a little uncertainly. "I do love singing gods. . . . But please, speak no more of head lopping and so on. Even if I could have, I never really meant to inflict *death* on Antonio and Alonso." He went into the lodge, tapping his brow.

Ariel fluttered her wings and looked after him in bafflement. Softly she asked, "What is death?"

CHAPTER 16

The Ruse

Prospero emerged from his house with his head bathed, combing his beard and bearing a tray of fruit, in time to catch Ferdinand and Miranda disappearing into the trees. "Halt!" he cried. He shook his staff at Ferdinand and said, "May I remind you of your vow, young sir! You signed a paper that promised you would leave untouched my daughter's virgin knot until you were well wed! And now I see you, creeping away like a villain, pulling her into the forest—"

"Forgive me, great magician." Ferdinand apologized, though in fact Miranda had been the one to propose the forest expedition. ("To pick berries," she had said demurely, batting her lashes and tugging at his sleeve.) "Please forgive me, sir," the

195

young man repeated. "Your fair daughter's skin is like ivory, her lips like cherries, her beauty beyond all compare, and because of it, my heart could not resist—"

"No more of that stuff!" Prospero growled. He placed the fruit on the ground and leaned his head on his staff as though smitten with migraine. "I begin to be sick of it. Only come back, and take your places—there." He raised his head and pointed with his staff to a spot in the dirt in the middle of the clearing. Immediately soft green grass covered the place, or so it appeared. Miranda and Ferdinand clapped their hands in delight, ran to it, and sat, though they looked disconcerted when they found that the ground was as hard as before. Miranda opened her mouth to protest, but Prospero overrode her complaint. He tossed the fruit at them. Miranda caught hers handily and laughed prettily when a banana bounced off Ferdinand's head.

"And now!" Prospero raised his staff to the sky. "Are you ready, my silly chick?" he whispered out of the corner of his mouth. Ariel whispered assent, and Prospero cried, "The Betrothal Entertainment!"

Ariel spoke a word.

From out of the freshwater spring flew Acrazia,

clothed as a goddess, in a shimmering robe of purple, blue, and green. Miranda and Ferdinand gasped and clapped, and even Prospero's tightly knit brow loosened in pleasure.

The sprite began to sing, and it seemed that he was accompanied by invisible instruments, by drums and harps and psalters and lyres, and all those who heard him were carried away by deep fancy. The sun shone through the latticed trees and dripped its gold on Prospero and Ferdinand and Miranda, and though none of them could later have said what Acrazia sang, they remembered what they felt as he sang it, a beautiful and terrible longing for something they could not name and that hung far out of reach. They pined for passionate embraces, for power to shed their heavy bodies and soar through the farthest reaches of the universe, past the sun and the moon and the stars. They did not know how long the spirit sang, for as they listened, spellbound, they forgot time. And when he ceased his song and vanished, the last note of the melody hung in the air for a long moment and kept them paralyzed with its beauty. When it faded, the three of them looked about them, and each saw that the others were crying.

"Ah, Ariel," Prospero murmured in a husky

voice. "How I fear you! But you have me in your grip. . . . Pray, continue. . . ."

Ariel spoke a second word.

Up through the ground, scattering pebbles and sand, shot Nous. Ferdinand started and fell back, and Miranda shrieked. The spirit took form in the air, turning from a cyclone to a shining yellow goddess, with hair of cornsilk and jeweled earrings that looked like red grapes, and a robe of green. He began his song, which was dark and earthy and rich as the loam of the clearing. And this song made them laugh and feel as though they were themselves gods and could do anything and do it perfectly, though when Prospero and Miranda and Ferdinand stood up and began to dance, they found that they did not dance well but moved as though they were drunk. They tripped over one another's feet and fell to the earth. But they did not care, for the song made them giddy, and they rolled about with spinning heads.

"Ah, my fine spirits," Prospero said, sitting up at last. "This is good, very good. Perhaps my spirits do better than I thought. Perhaps I will stay on this island forever! Such a brave entertainment. Pray, continue!"

Ariel spoke a third word.

With a rumbling like thunder, dressed in burnished gold armor and a helmet topped with high, stiffly towering horsehair, Fantasia rushed in from the sky.

Perhaps it was because he never finished his song, and because of the shocking rudeness with which it was interrupted, that the watchers could remember parts of it for the rest of their lives. The warlike spirit raised two mighty arms, and in a voice like boulders rolling down the mountainside, he began.

"Blessed daughter, blessed son, your fortune now
*   embrace,*
Children of great Prospero, and a chosen race!
Champions from the east are you, come this way
*   to rule,*
To seize this western island fair, to harvest every jewel,
Though you return to Milan, long your father
*   will rule here,*
No more to live on filberts, water scamels, and
*   small deer,*
With warriors he will conquer, and join both east
*   and west,*
Be worshiped by the lesser folk, who—"

"No!" Prospero rose in anger, shouting. "No, no, no, no!"

With a strange, hollow, and confused noise, the spirit vanished. The grass mirage under the young folk shrank, then disappeared entirely. Miranda and Ferdinand looked at Prospero and then at each other in amazement, as though they had just been awoken from a wondrous dream and were not sure where they were.

Prospero put a hand to his brow and leaned on his staff. "I should have known," he said angrily. "I should have known."

Ferdinand rose. "Great magician, these works have been glorious! Why did you halt them?"

Prospero smiled grimly. "I thank you, young man. But our revels now are ended. The sun sets. I suggest that you both retire to your beds." He pointed to the lodge and then to the empty hut of Caliban that stood apart from it. "Separately. You in the hut, Ferdinand."

An expression of distaste crossed the youth's face as he regarded the simple reed dwelling. He opened his mouth to speak but shut it when he saw Prospero's stern look. "Yes, sir." He kissed Miranda's hand, and looked a bit disconcerted at that hand's roughness. "Till the morrow."

The clearing was indeed gloomy in the evening light, with no fires lit, though the wide-open beach shone red-gold in the setting sun. Prospero walked out of the trees, trailed by Ariel, who was well out of sorts. "Master!" she called to him. "Why did you stop my last brave song? They were thrilled with it! Their eyes shone! And I saw your own eyes glitter."

"Yes!" Prospero turned on her in fury. "And that is why I stopped it! You feed us with airy dreams of power, and you never reckon the cost! I don't want to stay here and rule 'lesser folk.' I don't want to rule Milan! All I want is to go back to my farm, to see Althea and beg her forgiveness, though no doubt she's married again. And to see *Antonio* and beg *his*— Good God! Antonio! Where is he?"

"He wanders somewhere. It doesn't matter," Ariel said, laughing.

Prospero lunged at her. His arm went through her body. "Stop it or I will hate you!" he said, and shook an impotent fist. "Remember the gumbo-limbo tree! I will plague you with frogs—"

She laughed again, this time scornfully. "I begin to doubt your powers, master," she sang. "Have you any at all?"

"Oh, Ariel, *Ariel*! We've no time to quarrel!

Please, for the sake of our twelve-years' friendship, lead me with torches—imaginary torches, if they are all you can offer—but help me to find Antonio and Alonso and Gonzalo! There are dangers on the island, and *you knew it*, and—" He broke off and ran down the sand, toward the place where they had last seen the three men, in the cove by the quicksand marsh.

"What will you give me, master, for my help?" she sang behind him.

"Freedom!" he yelled back. "I will give you your freedom!"

"I begin to think I already have it," she whispered. But she flew after him, to see what would happen, and lit herself like a giant firefly to brighten their path.

He could not unmake her. She was beyond him. She felt powerful, still powerful, despite his troubling words and his loss of faith. Perhaps it was the mind of Gonzalo, that old dreamer, that fueled her brightness now.

And it was Gonzalo they heard first.

"It was a god, I tell you!" Gonzalo was shouting in the dark. "You men have no faith!"

"Faith in what?" came the vexed voice of

Antonio. "We may thank God the fellow came along to save us, but I assure you he was as human as we!"

"Human? He was divine! A dark spirit with eyes of fire, who came out of the air to pull us from quicksand to safety. Then he disappeared into the night, into thin air!"

"He ran out of the woods and then back into the woods," said Antonio. "He did *not* disappear. He was a man."

"What man would risk his own life to pull all three of us to the bank with only his two arms? Why, I was up to my waist, and you and Alonso were almost as far in! What man *could* have done it?"

"A very strong man," said Antonio. "And a brave one, and what's more a man with more common sense than all three of us put together. It was because you were staring at the ground searching for rubies that you stumbled into that marsh, and then we had to fall in trying to get you out! He knew better than we did, knew to tie himself fast to a tree before he reached out to us."

"He was a god!"

"Oh, *shut* your wine hole. I'm sick of your gabble! Ah, here's the beach, at last! How do you, Alonso?"

"You should have let me sink," groaned Alonso pathetically.

"Say nothing as I deal with these men," Prospero commanded Ariel in a low voice. He and his spirit stood by the bird rocks. "Only listen, my knavish chick, and follow us, invisibly, at a goodly distance. Or do you obey me no more?"

Ariel's wings hummed. She found the lost men's discourse entertaining and did not think she could bear to miss the shock of their meeting with Prospero. Despite what her master had just told her, she could not stop believing he would yet wreak a spectacular revenge on them. She began to blow toward him a fabulous picture of the beach exploding in fireworks, catapulting Antonio and Alonso up to the stars. But Prospero put up a hand, and the picture blurred at its edges and melted back into the air.

The three tired men suddenly emerged from the woods, looking dirty and pain wracked in the starlight. Antonio had lost his sword, Gonzalo had lost his hat, and they all had lost their boots. Alonso appeared to be sleepwalking as he mumbled, "My son, my son, my son! Ah, how will I tell your mother?"

"Courage, man!" Antonio slapped Alonso on the back. "We need water and food. I spy nests in these rocks. Let me climb up and—"

It was then that they saw Prospero, standing motionless by the rocks, lit by an eerie glow that seemed to come from nowhere. His hair and beard were wild and tangled from his run. He held a wooden staff before him, and his cloak billowed in the wind.

The three stopped short. Still weeping, Alonso crossed himself, and Antonio reached for a sword that wasn't there. Gonzalo fell to his knees and raised his hands to the sky. "Another god!" he cried. "Or a wizard!"

Prospero lowered his staff and leaned on it, smiling. "No, my foolish old friend," he said kindly. "Only a very bad farmer, who owns too many books."

CHAPTER 17

The Reunion

For a moment the three lost men were silent with amazement. Even Alonso ceased his sniffling and stared. Then Antonio walked slowly forward, his hands outstretched as if in supplication. In a voice of wonder, he said, "*Pros*pero?"

Prospero raised his own hand to stop his approach, and Antonio halted as though spellbound. "Yes, my brother, it is I," Prospero said. "But let us delay our embrace. I can no longer bear this poor man's misery. Alonso!"

The sound of Alonso's name broke the man's sad paralysis. "It *is* you!" he said, rushing toward Prospero and grasping his shoulder. "Good God, we thought you drowned these twelve years, though it was a puzzle that your body never washed up in

Portugal! And to think that you were blown *here*, in the middle of nowhere, and we to the same place! It is like—"

"Magic?" Prospero cocked an eyebrow. "An old wives' tale?"

Gonzalo had risen and was jumping up and down with delight, like a child. Antonio had been standing with his fists on his hips, shaking his head slowly and staring at his brother. Now he began to laugh. "Prospero! Magic! Ah, you and your mad book reading!" He sank to the sand in hilarity. "And you survived, for all your foolishness, though you could not even trim a sail! No doubt you read your way across the Atlantic, and your books washed up on this strange shore with you, and you spend your nights consulting them and commanding airy spirits to do your bidding!"

"Nothing so strange," said Prospero drily, trying to extricate himself from Alonso's embrace.

"Althea never gave up hope!" Alonso said. "I thought her as foolish as you! But now, as I think of my Ferdinand . . ." His face contorted, and a new sob threatened. "Do you remember my sweet little Ferdinand?"

"Ah, yes," said Prospero. "And I rejoice to tell

you that he is not drowned. He is, in fact, safe in slumber, hard by this beach, near my dwelling in the forest."

Alonso gave a cry of joy. "My son! Not dead! Oh, where?"

The first words of Alonso's sweet Ferdinand at being awoken from sleep by torch-bearing men were: "Where are my servants? Protect me!" When he saw that it was his own lost father who shook his shoulder, he said crossly, "Papa! So I do not yet own your lands!" But Alonso was too happy to be vexed by this remark. He folded Ferdinand in his embrace, saying, "Ah, the darling boy! And you *will* have a fine Arabian horse for your eighteenth birthday, and as many sugar dates as you can eat, once we get back to Milan!"

"Papa, I had the strangest dream, about a giant girl of the islands who bore wood on her back, as though she were a boy! And oddest of all, she seemed a peerless princess to me, though now, as I recall, her skin was rather freckled. . . ."

Prospero and Antonio left them rejoicing in the hut, where Gonzalo had fallen asleep despite their loud chatter, dreaming blissfully of rubies and diamonds and carbuncles the size of his head. The two brothers bore their torches out into the clearing.

"Back to Milan," said Antonio doubtfully. "If there were a way back!"

"There is a way back," said Prospero. "There are wonders yet to come." He knelt and rekindled the cook fire in the clearing, using his torch. Then he doused the torch in a bucket.

"Unless those wonders include a fully stocked ship, complete with sailors and a twenty-foot mast— We could build one, I suppose, in time. . . ." Antonio stroked his beard in thought. "But five men are few sailors."

"Five men and one woman."

Antonio dropped his hand. "Ah, this island woman of whom the youth in there babbles? I had assumed he was feverish."

"My daughter," Prospero said, a little huffily. "Your niece."

"My God," said Antonio slowly. "So Miranda lives too. My *God*! All of Althea's prayers answered!"

"And how—how is *she*?"

"Well. Helps in the running of the farm, now brimming with award-winning cattle and pigs. A prize cow this year at Lisbon! We've a fine business in livestock, which we share with Alonso. All of us have profited these twelve years. And the wine from our grapes—" He kissed his fingers and raised them to the air. "Famous as far as Portugal and Spain."

"Yes," said Prospero with a trace of bitterness. "You were always the capable one. Always the practical one, with the ideas. My disappearance has made you a wealthy man. Althea has married you, I suppose."

"Me? It was you she loved. She waits for you. Why would she marry me?"

For a moment Prospero could not speak. Then, in a shaky voice, he said, "Because I . . . failed her." He looked at his brother steadily. "And you."

Antonio laughed. "Brother, you weren't born to be a farmer; that's plain. But you gave your wife a fine daughter, and you pleased us all with your stories in the evenings. If you'd only let me make decisions and done what *I* said, we'd all have profited mightily, much sooner than we did."

Prospero was silent again. After a moment he said, "After two weeks at sea, I despaired. I looked at my foolishness, my poetry, my scanting of the farm and all the simple rules of common sense. I thought of Althea and you and even Alonso, and your vexation with me, and your—" He wiped his eyes with his hand and continued in unsteady voice. "Your hard work on our father's lands. You kept us from ruin. And I looked at my daughter, who laughed in the boat and trusted me. Wrongly."

Antonio patted Prospero on the shoulder and began to speak, but Prospero flinched and held up a hand. "Wait. I must tell you this. This knowledge—these memories—they were a worse torture than the sun and the storm and the thirst and even the trust on my little girl's face. And I could not bear them. I began to forget what had happened, what had *really* happened. I began to think you were the villain, and had set us adrift. 'Perfidious,' I said to myself. 'Antonio wants me dead and my only heir destroyed!' I saw a picture of your face, but it *wasn't* your face; it was the face of a devil. And then suddenly, strangely, I passed from a cloudy into a sunlit sea, as if over a line between worlds, and I found I believed my story utterly. And I fell asleep. And when I awoke"—he spread his arms widely—"here we were."

"It was a blessing that you landed anywhere," said Antonio gruffly.

"Perhaps," Prospero murmured. "Though I think whatever curse haunts mankind has its home in this place."

Antonio smiled and clapped Prospero's shoulder again. This time Prospero did not draw back. "Think not of curses now," Antonio said. "We live! And we'll build a new boat, and with our five men and one woman we'll find our way home. We saw another man, an islander. Do others dwell here, who might help us? Kindly disposed, that man seemed. Saved our lives!"

"Yes, I heard you speak of him," Prospero murmured distractedly. "The poor fellow . . . But I fear he'll never again be my friend." He looked at Antonio again. "Will you forgive me, my brother, and have me for a shipmate? Take me back to our farm, and I'll be happy to feed the pigs."

"A little pig feeding might help your soul." Antonio's voice was thoughtful. "But we would hate to lose your wild tales at the fireside. Work is good, but stories have their place."

"Though none will ever believe this one," said Prospero.

With a sudden sob, he hugged his brother, so tightly Antonio thought his bones would crack.

Had Ariel possessed a real stomach, she would have vomited. All these months, plotting the great revenge, and now—embraces! Granted, there was something romantic in this conclusion, but even its prettiness was marred by the talk of pig farms and—again—a cow!

She flew to the beach in disgust. Prospero had shrunk into an ordinary man. He was not a great hero, and she would no longer heed his commands.

It was as plain as the moonlight that cast its shining path on the water.

He had never been her champion from the east.

She folded her powers within herself like wings and brooded. Like the gathering tide, her magic rolled back from the woods and coves.

In an angle of the northeastern beach, the sailors awoke on the deck of Alonso's moored ship, to the creaking of ropes and the slap of water against the boat's wooden sides. They rubbed their eyes and looked about them in the darkness, asking one another what in the devil had happened to them and where they could possibly be.

Alonso and Ferdinand had fallen asleep in the hut, and though Prospero offered Antonio his own pallet in the lodge, Antonio said he was tired enough to rest happily on the ground. So Prospero left him there with a grass blanket and sat in his rough chair before his dwelling, perusing his books in the fading firelight.

Long, long, he read, till his eyes grew bleary and the letters seemed to come alive, and danced before his eyes. Wild tales of sea adventure, myths, fables, poetry . . . "The pages are crumbling anyway," he murmured sadly. "It is time to bury them for the worms. Yet, just one more story . . . just one more . . . and perhaps I might save the philosophy. . . ."

After many hours he rose and laid his books aside. "Good-bye, friends," he said.

Inside the hut, the embers of a fire still glowed. Miranda must have lit it. Near the fire, on a shelf, stood a bowl of his favorite filberts, which Miranda had gathered and left there that morning. There was little light in the lodge, and his eyes swam with the strain of reading, but he could just make out the shape of those delicious nuts. Amid the stresses of the day he had forgotten to eat, and at the sight of the filberts his stomach started to grumble. He reached for the bowl.

A stone flew out of the darkness and knocked the bowl to the floor, where the nuts scattered, pinks among reds. "Don't," a voice said grimly. "Those are unsorted. Have you not yet learned to shun poison?"

Prospero wheeled, nearly losing his balance. *"You!"*

Caliban limped into the firelight. "I meant to kill you with that very stone," he said. "But when I saw your silly face, I thought, why should I? I came across the ship that bore the sleeping sailors in the island's northeast nook. Then I saw your three fine friends, their faces as white as fishes' bellies. They will take you away, and soon you'll be gone. I'll have the place to myself without murdering you."

Prospero breathed out a long sigh and sank to the earth. He looked at Caliban in silence. Before him stood a well-muscled, dark-skinned youth, whose long black hair was clean, if it was tangled. He was bare chested and wore only a rabbit-skin cloth about his loins. His left leg twisted inward, but his back was straight.

"How could I ever have thought . . . ?" Prospero murmured.

Caliban glared at him. "You had best get on that ship when the bitch spirit brings it into the cove. I might change my mind about you. Remember that I'm a killer."

"You are no killer," Prospero said. "I've heard

the story of your mother's death, from Miranda. It was no murder. You were beset—well, we both know by whom. What's more, you saved three men's lives today."

"Four." Caliban bared his white teeth in a savage smile.

"Why did you do it?"

"I told you! To get you off the island. You can't sail by yourself; you can't do anything by yourself."

"Right." Prospero laughed ruefully. "Right you are."

"And as for saving *you*, I did it because—"

"I'm your father. The only one you'll ever know."

Caliban looked confused, and lapsed into silence.

Prospero bent forward and touched his knee. "Dear Caliban, I must ask forgiveness of many. Miranda, for one. But I have wronged *you* most of all. I wounded you. I've made a botch of our time on the island. Treating you like a pet, and then a slave; calling you a monster. I should have treated you like a son. I have thought much of it, these past days, especially this one, after I became reacquainted with . . . the other one." Dubiously Prospero regarded the banana-leaf document that lay at his elbow and at Ferdinand's signature, scrawled upon it.

"What other one?" asked Caliban.

Prospero made a dismissive gesture. "I will only say that as I regard you now, I think you much the better man."

Caliban had never before to his face been called a man. He seemed to grow an inch.

Prospero smiled at him and got to his feet. "I am glad you've returned." He patted his shoulder. "Stay on the island if you must. Go to the far side of it, and join those nameless people who beat their drums in the distance. Perhaps they'll be kinder to you than I have been."

Caliban thought for a moment, then said, "And perhaps not."

"The choice is yours. If you sail with us back to Milan, I will make you my heir. I have no son, after all. Nor does my brother. He's married to his vineyard. Milan is not so very far from the sea, though our Adriatic is colder than this strange nook of the Atlantic." He regarded Caliban in the flickering candlelight and smiled faintly. "If your feet could accustom themselves to shoes, you might be happy there. You would do well on our estates, and I would share with you everything I have."

"You have only one thing I want," said Caliban in a low voice.

"Ah." Prospero thought for a moment. Then he picked up the banana-leaf document and threw it in the fire. "This, again, was madness. Without the constant application of magic, my daughter's qualities are not likely to be appreciated by that young—"

"'Randa can topple a bird from a branch with a stone thrown from thirty paces!" Caliban said, his eyes shining. "And once we held a burping contest, and she won by ten full seconds!"

A rustle sounded from the darkness at the side of the lodge. "Who's . . . calling me?" Miranda sat up, shaking her red-blond hair, and peered into the fading circle of light cast by the fire. *"Caliban?"* She smiled broadly. "You've come home! Oh, my friend, I dreamed of the stupidest boy. . . ."

CHAPTER 18

Five Farewells

Only Gonzalo was disappointed when Alonso's vessel sailed trimly into their harbor the next morning at dawn. Though the ship still lacked one sail, its other three had been patched together by the mariners, who were so refreshed and happy to have lasted the storm that they felt like a hundred strong men, though they were only twelve. Some of them had caught fish off the island coast—so many that the nets had broken!—as well as a giant sea turtle, and the barrels on deck were still filled with storm water, and so they were well feasted and laughing when they rode into Prospero's cove.

Gonzalo's face fell, but it brightened again when Prospero told him that they might, after all, shipwreck on another magic island on their way back to

Italy, and if they did not, he himself would provide wild tales of his own travels and exile.

Antonio clucked his tongue at them and said, "Pish tush." What *he* wanted to know was where old clothes and stretched skins could be found on the island to stitch a new sail and, almost as important, whether their strongbox was still on board the ship. Yes, the sailors had found it, on the floor of the lower deck beneath the hatch, under the brackish seawater, as they bailed. The captain brought it to shore, and Antonio clutched it with glee, then opened it with a key he still wore about his neck. He showed his brother Prospero the silver coin they'd earned at the fair in Lisbon and the gold prize they'd won for their finest of cows, Princess Claribel, whom they'd sold afterward to an African king.

Prospero laughed till he cried, and called his brother the duke of Italian farmers.

By midafternoon they were almost ready to leave.

Caliban stood by the shore, looking resplendent but uncomfortable in silks and lace borrowed from Alonso's trunk, which had also survived the storm. He tugged at his collar and darted many surprised looks at his feet, which were now encased in velvet slippers.

Shoes had also been found for Miranda, among the sailors—her feet were rather large—and Antonio had given his niece a cape of sea-green satin, which set her eyes off well. She stood near her father, her reddish hair blowing wild about her face. Whenever her eyes met Ferdinand's, both of them looked away in embarrassment.

"He looks like the fool in my dream," Miranda murmured to Prospero.

"How singular!" Prospero patted her shoulder.

"I think I met that person yesterday, Papa," Ferdinand muttered to Alonso.

"You met her when she was two and you were four, in Milan," Alonso replied. "I remember it well. You quarreled over a box of sugarsops in Prospero's garden. You ate the bulk of them—quite rightly, a growing boy—and then she, naughty tot, rapped you over the head with the box."

Ferdinand frowned and raised a hand to his head in faint, painful memory and to shield it from the wind. He had twisted his hair around pinecones that morning, and his locks were once more curly. "She is *not* a nice girl, then," he said irritably. "Oh, I wish I had not lost my velvet cap in the storm! *When* will we be back in Italy?"

Miranda watched in pleased wonder as the captain

and two bearded, well-muscled young sailors readied the boat for the launch. "What are *those*?" she asked Prospero. "Oh, brave new world! May I meet them?"

Prospero shook his head. "I suggest that on this journey you stay close to our Caliban." He walked over to Caliban, who stood with his back to the sea, gazing back at the jungle. He put his hand on the youth's shoulder and said in a low, kind voice, "Do not weep. You bid farewell only to a mound of rocks. Her soul is no longer here. Perhaps, one day, after this strangest of lives, you will meet her again."

Caliban wiped the wet from his cheek. "I laid honeysuckle on her grave this morning. So hard to think it will be the last time!"

"We will make her a memorial in Milan." Prospero patted his shoulder. "This I promise."

Caliban could not speak, but he nodded his thanks.

"You should see to Miranda." Prospero looked at his daughter, who was now exchanging wide smiles with the burliest of the sailors. "She's in your keeping now." He sounded faintly relieved. "Don't let her forget that your friendship is the oldest one she has. In the end she will honor it."

At that moment Miranda glanced at Caliban, who was looking at her as he pulled his lace collar. She smiled. Caliban raised his eyebrows and pointed at her new canvas shoes, and the two of them walked toward each other, laughing.

A gleam of white near a boulder caught Prospero's eye. He walked toward it, bent down, and picked up a brittle fragment of a bone. "You!" he said pityingly and companionably. Then he strolled back into the woods, toward the clearing. "Three things more."

A half hour later he brushed his hands from the new mound of dirt he'd piled, hard by the grave of Sycorax. "Rest in peace, old fellow, at last," he told Jasper's bone, now a foot deep in the earth. "May you find your Promised Land." He placed a sand dollar on the mound and rose. "Two things more."

Behind his empty lodge he dug a deeper and wider grave and cast into it those books he had once held to be sacred. Above them he piled sand and soil, until the hole was level with the ground. Then he sat on his knees, sweating, and regarded the flat earth morosely.

"Buried," he whispered sadly. "All buried. I

could barely read them anymore, with their crumbling edges and their blotchy ink and their water stains. It is best now. Let words feed the worms."

He wiped the soil from his hands and stood. "One thing more."

He found her, as might be expected, in the last place he looked. She was sitting motionless, wings folded, in the charred fork of the ruined gumbo-limbo tree.

He knelt. He took off and folded his many-colored robe and laid it on the earth. On top of it he placed his staff. He had hung a second sand dollar about his neck with twine, as a last remembrance of the island, and its round whiteness contrasted starkly with the browned skin of his grizzled chest. He touched the dollar, looking tired.

"Ariel," he said softly, "I am going."

"I know," she whispered.

"Do you want to know why?"

"No," she sang sweetly. "I don't care. Perhaps you could leave Gonzalo."

He laughed sadly. "He dreams of staying, but he'll come with us. Ah, my chick! Do I dare look in your eyes again?"

Those purple orbs glowed at him. Her wings still

lay motionless on her back, but her seaweed hair blew dreamily about her head.

He shook his own head, gazing at her. With difficulty, he turned his eyes to the human group clustered about the launch, enjoying a last island meal of roasted tubers, spiced with sea salt. Then he looked down at his folded robe, whose weather-stained fabric now seemed to him plain and dull. He glanced back at her, and she shimmered, as bright as before.

"You are beautiful," he said. "And your mind is keen. But you never truly understood me, or any of us. Your world is all colors, but when you look at us, you see only black and white. Our hearts are not so simple, my dear. In the end you know only our surfaces, and you offer us no wisdom."

She blinked her gorgeous eyes. "What will I do, now that you are gone?" she said, in frank curiosity.

He wiped moisture from beneath his eyes. "I thank you, Ariel, for the way you have brightened my life. Yet you made me forget things I should not have forgotten and blinded me to things I should have seen. Despite your glory, you have done much harm. What will you do without me? you now ask.

Not very much, if I have any power at all." He rose, holding his staff. His face was contorted with sadness.

Her own face stayed unmoved, and its silver surface shone. "You do *not* have any power. And you are not my champion."

"True." He nodded. "These things you have rightly guessed. But there is a power above me—"

"Setebos?" she asked, on her guard. She raised her wings slightly.

He shook his head. "*I* call this power God, and I have spoken to him too seldom on this island. I could not kill you, even if I wished to." His voice broke. "But perhaps God will give me enough magic, here at the last, to put you to sleep."

"Another tale of your brother's cattle-breeding schemes would do that." Ariel yawned delicately.

In tears, Prospero laughed.

Then he broke his staff.

The two halves of blackened wood rolled on the sand, and for a moment they seemed to writhe like snakes. He put his foot on them. Once more he fingered the sand dollar, whose four splayed oval holes formed a natural cross on its white surface. He bowed his head and silently prayed.

Then he raised his chin and turned to go. "Good-bye." After a step he paused and looked back over his shoulder. "I have loved you, Ariel."

He walked down to the launch. With the rest of the group he entered the boat, and the sailors pushed them into the bay, then climbed in, their breeches dripping. Miranda and Antonio and Caliban helped ply the oars as they rowed. Ferdinand sat in the prow, wiping seaweed from his shoes.

When they reached the big ship, the nine of them climbed aboard the vessel and clasped hands with the sailors who waited there. They pulled anchor. A stiff breeze puffed their patched sails, and they tacked through blue waters toward the darkening east.

The boat grew smaller in the distance as they approached the edge of the Triangle. A heaviness came over Ariel, and her lids drooped over her purple eyes. Still she watched, as if through a haze. And impossible though it seemed—for the humans were now many leagues distant, and their bark was a speck—she thought she saw Prospero in the prow, as the ship burst through the rim of enchanted air into gray skies and choppy waters. Without his staff, the

227

wise man stood straight on the pitching deck and laughed, and lifted his arms to embrace the rain he had not made.

Back on her sunlit beach, Ariel rested in the shell of the gumbo-limbo tree.

"What is love?" she murmured drowsily.

Then she closed her eyes.

He Comes

What are the dreams of a dream?

Pictures seen and sounds heard as if under water, distorted and dim. In Ariel's painless sleep she saw the blended colors of two hundred thousand sunsets. She heard the muffled cries of seabirds and the endless breaking of waves on the beach.

She was a brittle bone, a drop of water, a bird's wing. She changed into a million forms, as did the others who floated through her dreams.

Her memory gave her Prospero's face. *You were not my champion*, her mind whispered. *No conqueror of my island*. The face melted into those of other humans who had failed her: Caliban, and Sycorax, and Jasper, who had no sooner birthed her than he'd fled his own body.

None of you were my champions, her sleeping mind whispered. *But my champion will come.*

A hundred years passed, and another hundred.

During six slow-rolling centuries the drums still sounded from the western part of the island. Sometimes she heard them every day. At other times months passed without their throbbing. For two hundred years they did not sound at all, and then they returned. But for Ariel, the drumming was always there, in her mind. In her sleep as in her waking, she knew nothing of time.

She waited.

In her dream she became dimly aware that the Triangle was shrinking. Its base still ran across the island, but as the isosceles shape's long sea legs moved inward, its base also came closer, moving down the mountains behind her toward the eastern beach where she slept. With it came the drums. They grew louder.

Gradually, still dreaming, she came to feel the presence of other spirits, western spirits, spirits who were unknown to her and owed her no service. They belonged to the people who beat the drums. If they reached her cove and her tree and found her helpless and alone, she knew she would disappear.

Save me, she whispered urgently as she slept. *Come, my champion from the east! Together we will cross the mountains, and none will stand in our way. Come, my champion from the east!*

And he came.

On a night in autumn—though the island knows nothing of seasons—the boats sailed into her cove. Anchors dropped, and the ships sat in silence but for a hymn that rose from the throats of the sailors on their decks. The music stirred her. The Latin words crept into her ears, and her drowsy thoughts shook themselves, like seabirds rising.

After two hours the sun came up from the eastern sea and shone on the red crosses that adorned the boats' huge sails. Dawn lit the ships' painted names. *Niña. Pinta. Santa María.*

A dinghy was lowered and rowed to shore. It ground to rest on the sand. He jumped out and walked through the water, his soldiers behind him. They carried metal sticks and leather bags filled with gunpowder, and their faces were shrouded by helmets. But he was bareheaded and bore only a sheathed sword.

He stepped firmly onto the beach, then knelt to kiss the ground. Standing, he raised his sword to the sky and cried, "By the grace of God, I claim this island for the glory of Holy Spain!"

She awoke.

From the tree where she sat she could see him clearly. His eyes were as blue as the eyes of Sycorax, and his head held a thousand dreams. He was tall and blocked the sun, which cast its rays in his wake, so the light formed a halo behind his head.

She too grew tall, as strength welled inside her. She spread her wings, flew down the beach, and hovered on the sand before him.

When his blue gaze met her purple one, she hung their shared visions in the air. For an instant the placid sky was filled with dark demons and pale gods, with burning mountainsides and exploding trees. Swords shone and guns flared as half a million warriors, some painted and naked, some clothed in metal skins, yelled in a babble of tongues as they clashed to the glorious songs of war. And above the musical fray this blue-eyed man stood triumphant, holding aloft his silver-hilted blade.

The vision faded. She smiled and leaned close to the wide, wondering eyes of Cristóbal Colón.

"Come, my lord," she hummed in his ear. "Let's march inland."